NIGHT FLYERS

ALSO BY MICHAEL NEWTON

Gideon Thorn

Skinwalker

Leviathan Rising

Ghost Town

Mountain Devils

Soul Slayers

Hallowed Ground

NIGHT FLYERS

A WEIRD WESTERN

GIDEON THORN
BOOK 7

MICHAEL NEWTON

Night Flyers
Paperback Edition

Dark Wolf Books
An Imprint of Wolfpack Publishing
1707 E. Diana Street
Tampa, FL 33610

www.darkwolfbooks.com

Paperback ISBN 979-8-89567-607-3
Ebook ISBN 979-8-89567-606-6

In Memory of Bill Crider (1941-2018) and the VBKs. Rest in peace, friend.

NIGHT FLYERS

PROLOGUE

BEAR VALLEY, ARIZONA TERRITORY: FEBRUARY 14, 1877

Something was after Simon Cain's livestock. The cattle woke him shortly after midnight, squealing panic from the barn, with his mutt Rusty yapping up a storm besides.

"I'm coming, dammit!" Cain bawled out to no one in particular, rising from bed in his long underwear and pulling on his well-worn boots, forgoing any other clothing as he lit a lamp and clomped out toward the main room of his farmhouse, parlor and a kitchen-dining room rolled into one.

He saw no point in dressing any further, since he lived alone, expected to find nothing but coyotes in dark outside —and if a human had come trespassing, so what? He didn't owe the sneaky bastard any dressing up before he opened fire.

Cain took his eight-gauge Greener double-barreled shotgun from its place over the hearth and checked—no need, but it was habit—to make sure it was loaded: birdshot in the right-hand barrel, buckshot in the left, leaving the hammers down for now. The Greener also chambered solid slugs, tipping the scales at eighty-one grams, used for hunting elephants and such in Africa, but he preferred the shotgun shells.

He also kept a Colt revolver in the nightstand drawer, beside his lonely bed, but he preferred the Greener for its noise and wallop after dark, when aiming could be dicey for him. Nothing he'd encountered in the territory so far could survive a square hit from the Greener, and its *boom* alone was commonly enough to put most species on the run. As for the shotgun's brutal kick, Cain seldom tried to aim it from his shoulder, knowing it would leave a painful bruise. Better, he'd found, to wedge the stock against his hip and shoot from there, letting the recoil spin him halfway round, while anything in front of him was blown to smithereens.

Admittedly, Bear Valley had its share of predators, beginning with the bruins that it had been named for, going down the scale from there to cougars and coyotes, badgers and bobcats, javelinas that would gore you if you gave them half a chance, on down to Gila monsters, rattlesnakes and coral snakes, then tarantulas and scorpions.

Cain worried more about two-legged predators, living this close to Mexico and in an area used commonly for bandits, rustlers, and assorted hostile Indians in transit, headed north or south. Aside from native Navajo and Chiricahua, Yaqui from Sonora also tended to regard the border as a vague suggestion. Then, Cain also had to think about the so-called "friendly" Papago—or Tohono O'odham, as they preferred to call themselves—penned up for three years now on one of Uncle Sam's bleak reservations, sprawling over some 4,400 square miles of desert.

Too many bad hombres around who'd love to raid his stock, cart off supplies, or maybe just kill Cain and torch his buildings for the hell of it.

No moon was visible tonight—ironic, when you thought about it, since today was Valentine's Day, when young lovers were supposed to be out spooning underneath the open sky. Some wily printer in New England had begun cranking out cards for the occasion thirty-odd years back, but Simon Cain ignored that kind of folderol.

Besides, you had to love someone before it started making sense.

Cain stepped down from his porch, then stood stock-still under the vast night sky. Whatever had disturbed his cattle in the barn and woken him, the beasts were quiet now. Maybe a mountain lion passing by, he thought, deciding that it couldn't breach the barn.

Still, he was up now, with his gun and lamp. It only made good sense to take a closer look.

There were no padlocks on the barn, no need for special keys. Cain kept the doors barred after nightfall, and the cattle—as they'd proved tonight—were all the burglar alarm he needed. Not much got them riled, but when they were...

A *whop-whop* flapping noise somewhere above Cain him made him pause, head tilted back, searching the sky. He raised his lamp first, but it only ruined his night vision, so he lowered it. Was that something retreating, blotting out the stars?

Impossible.

The territory claimed two kinds of eagles, bald and golden, but he'd never seen or heard of either with a wing-span more than seven feet or so. This thing was double that, unless—

"Unless it was your goddamned fool imagination," Simon muttered to himself, and started moving toward the barn once more.

Even a condor, if you glimpsed one in the territory, shouldn't have so great a wingspan, and from what Cain understood, they didn't fly by night. What would've been the point, when even keen eyes couldn't spot a meal of carrion in darkness?

Cain reached the barn, set down his lamp and weapon to remove the wooden plank securing double doors. Opening one side, all that he needed at the moment, still required two hands, but once he'd hauled it back enough to walk inside, he grabbed the light and shotgun, thankful for the warm glow that surrounded him and pushed the shadows back.

Inside, Cain stopped again. Not only were the cattle silent now, but he could see them lying in their stalls on beds of straw, sleeping as if they'd never been disturbed and cried for him at all.

"The hell?" he asked, but no one answered him.

It wasn't like his stock spoke English, but he'd thought the lamplight and his voice would rouse a sleeping steer, at least. And how could all of them fall back asleep so quickly, when they'd been raising a ruckus not ten minutes earlier?

Cain meant to take a closer look and find out for himself.

Veering off toward the right-hand row of stalls, he muttered, "Wakey wakey now. You can't just roust me outa bed and—"

Cain stopped short, peering into the nearest stall. His lamplight glistened redly, and he clearly smelled the sickly sweet, metallic scent of blood.

"Christ's sake!" he swore.

The steer was dead, a yawning throat wound drooling crimson, but its heart no longer pumped a steady flow. And still, the other stock was quiet as a grave.

Cain felt a pounding in his temples as he moved from one stall to the next, lamp raised, and found more steers laid out and leaking into sodden straw. All dead, but he could see that none of them were butchered in the normal sense. Each had its throat torn open, but the closer Cain examined them, he realized there should have been *more* blood.

A great deal more, in fact. Each cow had roughly ten gallons of blood inside it. Multiplied by thirty head, that made three hundred gallons, give or take. The barn's floor should have been awash in crimson, Cain's boots squelching in it, but in no case had a stain escaped from any of the stalls.

"What, in the name of God?"

Cain hadn't been the praying sort since he had gone out on his own, around sixteen, and wasn't starting now. Assuming he believed in God at all—a big "if"—no one in his right mind would ascribe this wanton slaughter to the Lord.

So then, what?

As he stood clueless between the silent rows of stalls, something shifted and made a rustling noise above him, from the hayloft. His chickens couldn't make it up there, with their wings clipped, but pigeons tried to roost among the bales from time to time, and once he'd scared a red-tailed hawk that had been checking out his barnyard hens. This sounded *bigger,* though, almost as if a man were scuffling around, not bothering to hide the fact.

Well, if it *was* a man who'd killed his stock, Cain didn't care whether the prick was white, black, brown or red. He owed Cain better than twelve hundred dollars for his steers —that, or his life.

"Come down from there, you sumbitch!" Cain demanded, startled and a bit embarrassed by the tremor in his voice. "And I mean show yourself *right now!*"

Instead, whoever—*what*ever—was up there made a kind of creaking noise, like big old rusty hinges might've done.

Cain set his lantern down and clutched the Greener in both hands, thumbing its double hammers back and drawing comfort from their sound. He raised the weapon, more than ready to accept its recoil for a chance at bringing down the prowler in his loft.

"I have to come up there and getcha, you'll be goddamned sorry!" he announced. No quaver that time, thankfully, although his hands were definitely trembling now.

Nothing from the loft, except another heavy shifting sound and that damned rusty-hinge creaking again.

"Okay, then. If you'd rather die than show your face—"

And then, it did.

Was that a face? Cain wondered, blinking in the lamplight. And if so, what in hell ever possessed a visage like that one, so large and hideous?

Cain fired his load of birdshot, staggered from the Greener's kick, and knew that he was falling when he let the buckshot fly. It was a clean miss with the second barrel, anyway, and likely both of them. He landed on his backside, all the wind knocked out of him, so that he couldn't scream, much less plead for his life,

Above him, a vast shadow launched from the hayloft, swooping down to smother him.

ONE

PIMA COUNTY, ARIZONA TERRITORY: MARCH 2, 1877

The wooden sign was roughly three feet wide and two feet high, nailed to a sturdy post beside a road rutted with wagon tracks. Whoever made it had painted "MONTANA CAMP" in black, the words now sun-fading toward gray.

The painter hadn't mixed up his or her geography. Montana Territory lay nine hundred miles or so due north, but this Montana Camp was named after Montana Peak, a 5,300-foot mountain that loomed above the town and was responsible for its existence, miners toiling to extract its gold, silver, copper, lead and zinc.

Gideon Thorn knew that because he always did his homework prior to taking on a job that might wind up being his last.

At twenty-five and counting, Thorn had seen more than his share of sudden death and dealt out some of it himself. He never took a moment of his life for granted, but he didn't let fear slow him down, either.

He'd come by train as far as Tucson, seventy miles north of where he sat astride his gray stallion, Shadow. A fair rope's length behind him stood his molly pack mule, Bell, wearing its normal bored expression. The ride south had consumed five days, and all of them were ready for a roof over their heads, someplace to eat and sleep that wasn't constantly exposed to desert winds.

Thorn's journey had begun in Provo, Utah, where he'd tried to follow up on claims of that some strange creature called the *shunka warakin*—"carries off dogs," translated from the native dialect—had added humans to its night-time menu. Thorn hadn't resolved that mystery, although he'd found and measured pawprints roughly cougar-size, but with the oval shape of canine tracks, with six pads rather than the cougar's five and claw marks always visible, not sheathed like a feline's.

He might go back to try again on that some other time, but since the two dead men reported locally had been exposed to scavengers for several days before their bodies were recovered, Thorn thought it was sixty-forty that their wounds were caused by vultures or coyotes.

Whatever was troubling Montana Camp, he thought, was something else.

He clucked and gave Shadow a gentle heel, reaching out with his mind at the same time to tell the stallion and his mule, *It's time to go.* Belle gave back her version of a yawn, but fell in step as Shadow took the lead.

A letter from the marshal of Montana Camp, one Lute Brisbin, had reached Thorn on the eve of his departure from Provo, planning on a run to South Dakota, where there'd been reports of deaths preceded by sightings of what some Badlands homesteaders were calling a banshee. Brisbin's letter had trumped that job, referring to slew of mutilated livestock and four human victims, all missing most of their blood. The county sheriff, Brisbin said, had placed the blame of desert predators and scavengers that came along behind them, but the marshal had his doubts.

Thorn wondered how Brisbin had heard of him, unstated in his letter, but he guessed the lawman must've read some story in the papers, likely penned by Dinah Pilcher. Thorn had met the lady journalist nine months ago, when he'd been tracking down a cult that practiced human sacrifice in California's San Diego County. They'd survived that outing, touch-and-go though it had been, and Dinah had come back into his life while he was scouring Summit County, Colorado, for the beast that slew his parents back in 1854, when Thorn was two years old.

That night had left him with a scar across his scalp, the hair around it snow-white in shocking relief against the rest, which was as black as Thorn's daily attire: a wide-brimmed had, frock coat and vest, trousers and knee-high boots. Only his shirts were white, worn with a black string tie.

The second time around with Dinah had been even closer, both of them marked down as dinner by a hulking thing that took more killing than a rogue grizzly. Again, they had pulled through, and Thorn had grudgingly agreed to let her write his story based on interviews conducted over several weeks in Denver, and while traveling. They'd spent some heated nights together, too, before Dinah told him she craved getting to work again, and so had parted company.

Too bad, Gideon thought, but at the same time, he knew just what Dinah meant. They both had jobs to do, and neither one of them was cut out for a settled life.

Thorn took his time as he approached Montana Camp,

a rough-hewn, bustling town with three saloons, one freshly painted Baptist church, and sundry shops lining its dusty central street. Founded in 1870—more homework there—the settlement had something like a thousand residents, with rugged men outnumbering the women five or six to one. That kept the soiled doves busy in their cribs upstairs, over the barrooms, and Thorn guessed that Marshal Brisbin spent most of his time on drunks and brawlers.

Until recently, that is.

Gideon's life was hectic, but he tried to keep the small things orderly, at least. Therefore, his first stop was the Copper Queen hotel, where he was greeted by a long-faced clerk somewhere in his mid-forties, booking three nights with an option to stay longer if he let them know ahead of time. After he'd stashed his long guns and his saddlebags upstairs, the stout door double-locked, he'd taken Belle and Shadow two blocks to the livery and left them with a hostler who appeared to know what he was doing, making sure the guy knew Thorn intended on returning daily, checking in.

By then, he'd spied the marshal's office, next-door to the undertaker's parlor, but a growling stomach sent Thorn to the larger of Montana Camp's two restaurants, the Mother Lode. A waitress with more freckles than he'd ever seen before spent half a minute eyeing him—six-four, tipping the scales around 170, wearing twin Colt Peacemakers and a Bowie knife around in back, a smaller dagger's handle showing from the top of his right boot—and seated him alone, table for two, where he could gaze out through a window at the street.

She blinked when Thorn took off his hat, showing the white streak in his hair, but shook it off and said, "Our menu's on the wall. I'd recommend the steak or stew, but stay clear of the fish."

"The stew it is," he told her. "And some coffee, please."

"Coming right up," she answered back, and risked a smile.

Thorn counted seven other diners in the restaurant, a bit past midday, two couples and three men eating alone. One of the women looked him over, frowning slightly, but the others didn't seem to pay him any mind.

The stew was piping hot and plentiful, with biscuits on the side. Thorn dug in with a will, glad to discover there was no shortage of tender beef amidst the carrots and potatoes, peas and onions, all combined with thick, rich gravy. He'd declined milk with his coffee, pleased to find it rich and strong. The biscuits, made with buttermilk, were hot enough to melt the pats of butter Thorn applied to them.

So far, so good, he thought, taking his time over the meal while he reviewed what else he knew about Montana Camp.

The town had a crime rate commensurate with other mining settlements its size, most spinning off from booze, card tables, or the hookers' cribs. Claim-jumpers seemed to be under control, the miners watching out for one another with regard to strangers, and the odd horse thief was either hanged or sent to Yuma Territorial Prison after a speedy trial. Whatever else was going on, it hadn't made the newspapers in Tucson or Phoenix so far, and Thorn found that a tad suspicious in itself.

What else?

There was no hint of any precious metals playing out within the lifetimes of the town's existing miners, which meant population growth, more buildings, possibly a school as families moved in with kids or couples already in residence began to pop them out. In time, Thorn knew the larger mining companies would notice what was going on, step in, and try to put the squeeze on independent small-timers.

That wasn't his problem. His interest lay altogether elsewhere.

From the night his parents and his older brother had been mauled to death, Thorn reckoned that his course in life was set, although he hadn't known it at the time.

Six months or so after his loss, he'd been extracted from an orphanage in Lawrence, then in Kansas Territory, now famous for being raided by Quantrill's Raiders back in 1853. The agent of his personal salvation had been Aunt Drusilla Thorn, with Gideon, the last survivors of their line. She hadn't made the trip herself, of course, but rather sent Obi Magoro, once her late father's manservant, brought back from western Africa to Russell Thorn's mansion on Beacon Hill, in Boston.

With the old man's death, Drusilla and Obi stayed on, and Gideon became her legal ward. She'd paid his way through Weatherford Academy and Harvard University, where Gideon pursued "liberal arts," including anthropology and history; biology, zoology and botany; comparative religions and classical literature, earning his B.A. at twenty-one.

Before then, he'd learned other things, as well. When schoolyard bullies tagged him as a runt, Obi Magoro had instructed Thorn in Africa's martial arts—Dambe bare-knuckle boxing, Engolo ritual combat, and Nguni stick-fighting—so that his enemies left him alone. At home, he also was exposed to Aunt Drusilla's avid Spiritualism, absorbed first-hand from occultist and personal acquaintance Paschal Beverly Randolph, famed for his skill with tarot cards and ouija boards.

Before proceeding on to Harvard Law and what he had supposed would be a lucrative but dull career in Boston or Manhattan, Thorn had accepted the gift of a summer in Europe, cut short by a telegram announcing his aunt's demise. Back in the only home he'd ever really known, Gideon found himself sole heir to the Thorn family fortune, administered for years by Messrs. Block, Enright & Sloan. The terms of Aunt Drusilla's will provided Obi Magoro a home on Beacon Hill for the rest of his life, and Gideon wouldn't have had it any other way. As for himself...

With money readily on tap and nagging questions from his youth unanswered, he had undertaken what he thought of as a private odyssey, roaming the nation—chiefly to the West, but ultimately without limit—in pursuit of natural or *super*natural anomalies that posed a threat to other lives and families. Along the way so far, he had encountered human monsters and some altogether different kinds, even a real-life dragon in a Texas mining town much like Montana Camp, and just last year he had achieved a kind of closure for the trauma of his youth, with aid from Dinah Pilcher and his lifelong friend, Obi Magoro.

While he searched, Thorn took advantage of his childhood gift for silent interaction with some animal species, though others couldn't understand him or, perhaps, simply refused to answer. As his backup, he maintained a bevy of eclectic knowledge and a small but lethal arsenal that he wasn't afraid to use on man or beast at need.

Aside from what he carried on his person day to day, Thorn also packed an 1872 Sharps rifle in .50-90 caliber, accurate beyond a thousand yards with its custom scope attached. His other long gun was a Winchester Model 1873 lever-action rifle, loading fifteen of the same .44-40 rounds Thorn carried in his Colt revolvers.

All of that had stood him in good stead so far, despite a few close brushes with the Reaper; those things and Thorn's capacity for opening his mind to new ideas and possibilities. He had long since accepted that, while common explanations were the best and easiest, once they had been ruled out, he had to look for something else.

For Gideon, that open-mindedness didn't translate into what some folks called religious conviction. Aunt Drusilla's bent toward the occult and outré had inoculated Thorn against the pulpit-pounding frauds who wished damnation on their neighbors if said neighbors failed to drop in every Sunday, filling the collection plates. Instead, he'd sampled all major religions academically, retaining what he found worthwhile from each, discarding what he knew to be the propaganda of hypocrisy.

Around his neck and out of sight beneath his shirt, Thorn wore a silver chain bearing a small cross, a Star of David, a crescent moon of Islam, a pentagram of Wicca, and a feather for diverse American native religion. He didn't flaunt those symbols, and was wise enough to keep them strictly out of site during his recent trip to Utah, where the Mormon sect essentially ran everything.

No true believer, Thorn, but neither did he make a conscious point of rubbing others the wrong way. They were entitled to their notions, even to their fantasies—at least, until the moment when they made the grave mistake of getting on his bad side, taking Thorn for someone they could push around.

Gideon had left room for dessert and tried the apple pie, which proved to be as tasty as his stew and biscuits, topped with cheddar cheese that took him by surprise at first, but which he found delectable. He finished off the pie, together with a second cup of coffee, paid his tab and left a dollar tip for his waitress, who grinned at him to beat the band.

Outside, the day was winding down, at least for merchants who were slowly closing up their shops. Montana Camp's saloons—the Dry Gulch, Lucky Strike, and Gold Dust—were just ramping up as afternoon began its fade to dusk, music from out-of-tune pianos jangling from behind their batwing doors. Thorn saw work-weary men approaching each saloon in turn, greeted by women's laughter in one case, and in another by applause.

Some local hero, Gideon surmised, deciding he could do without a drink or three his first night in Montana Camp.

Glancing off toward the marshal's office, Thorn saw no lights showing from inside. Tomorrow morning would be soon enough, he thought, and turned back toward the Copper Queen hotel and bed.

He'd covered half a block, passing an alley's mouth, when someone standing in the shadows there spoke up. "Gideon Thorn?"

Thorn swiveled toward the sound, his right hand settling on a Peacemaker's curved grip, thumb flicking off the holster's hammer thong.

"Whoa! Easy there," the stranger said. He stepped into the waning light of afternoon, the glimmer on his vest a lawman's badge.

"Marshal Brisbin?"

"The very same. You made fair time from Provo, Mr. Thorn."

"I do my best," Gideon said. "How did you spot me?"

"*No problemo,*" Brisbin answered him. "You look just like your photograph."

TWO

"My photograph, you say?" Gideon hoped he hadn't sounded too surprised.

"Sure. In the newspaper." As he replied, Brisbin stepped closer, offering his hand, and Thorn shook it. He noted that the marshal wore a Smith & Wesson Model 3 Schofield revolver low on his right hip, tied down.

"Which newspaper might that be, Marshal?"

"Call me Lute. And that would be the *Tucson Citizen*. It's pretty much the only paper we get here, although I hear they plan on starting up another daily soon."

"About this photograph..."

"Came with the article about you, Sir. The story is what set me thinking you might know a way to solve our problem, if you felt like helping out. And here you are."

"I got your letter," Thorn replied. "It was a trifle vague."

Brisbin nodded. "I didn't want you thinking I was on the locoweed."

"I like to hear the facts before I judge."

"Sounds good to me."

"About this photograph and story—"

Brisbin interrupted him. "You want to step down to my office for a drink while we palaver? It'll save us shouting over what passes for music in our local sporting houses."

"Fine. Now, Marshal—"

"Lute."

"Okay, Lute. I'm not used to being in the press."

That wasn't strictly true, of course. Some of his work had rated mention in newspapers, usually with the stranger parts toned down or left out altogether. More than once, his name was only cited as a drifter who'd been asked to leave one hamlet or another when the dust settled and local lawmen tried to put a lid on what had happened.

"Well, Sir—"

"Might as well be 'Gideon'."

"Well, Gideon, it was a sort of interview. The lady who reported it—"

"Was Dinah Pilcher," Thorn completed Brisbin's thought for him. He saw it all as plain as day now, though he hadn't read the article himself. She'd published more then one, acknowledged in the last letter Dinah had written to him, and he'd posed—reluctantly—for what was more or less a formal photographic portrait.

Now, he was about to find out if that notice in the press had helped or hurt him. Clearly, Marshal Brisbin was about to pitch a job, but Gideon still didn't know if Lute had jumped the gun, or if he was, in fact, some kind of mental case.

"Miss Pilcher," Brisbin echoed. "She's the very one. It sounded like she knew you pretty well."

Including biblically, Gideon thought, but kept that to himself. He settled for, "We did a bit of work together, when she didn't know what she was getting into. After, she was...interested, you could say. There was some talk about a book, but we've been out of touch a while. I doubt that anything will come of it."

They reached the marshal's office and Lute plied his key. "I wouldn't be so sure about that, Gideon. The article I read, she still had hopes of telling what she called your 'whole story'."

"Few would believe it," Thorn opined.

"But, then again," said Brisbin, as he lit a lamp and took a whisky bottle from a desk drawer, setting up two glasses, "some just might."

Thorn took a seat across the desk from Brisbin, sipped his drink, and found it to be aged bourbon.

"Which brings us to your problem."

"Oh, I'd say it's more than just a *problem*. It started out with livestock, steers and sheep on some outlying ranches, killed by no means I can figure out. They're mauled like some wild animal got hold of them, mostly with throats torn open, but they're missing nearly all their blood, aside from some spilled on the ground when they were bitten."

"When you say it started out with stock..."

"I mean we've lost four people now, two ranchers plus the wife to one of them, and a night watchman out at the Elvira mine. That's north of town a mile or so."

"And the other attacks?"

"Spread all over the place, no pattern to them I can see."

"No disrespect," Thorn said, "but this sounds like a matter for the county sheriff, possibly the state police."

"No offense taken, and you're right. Thing is, we've got no state police these days, not since the Territorial Rangers packed up in 1862. As far as Pima County goes, it's one of only four counties established at the Gadsden Purchase, back in '53. It covers more than twenty-one thousand square miles right now. The legislature talks about some other counties breaking off from it, but they've done nothing yet."

"The sheriff?" Gideon prodded.

"That's Charles Shibell. Age thirty-five the last I heard, so I've got half a dozen years on him, but he's the one who got elected. Been to college up in Iowa, then clerked a while in Sacramento, at a general store, before he came down here. Married Mercedes Sais Quiroz in '68, kidnapped by the Apaches from Green Valley when she was a kid, before the Civil War. She bore four children with Shibell, then gave it up and died last year, just twenty-six years old. He'll likely get remarried, since the voters like a settled man in charge of law and order, right?"

"Speaking of which..."

"The charitable view is that Sheriff Shibell has plenty on his plate, trying to run a county bigger than Vermont and Massachusetts put together, outlaws everywhere you look, all kinds if rustlers, renegades and border trash."

"And what's *your* view, leaving aside the charity?" Thorn asked.

"Shibell's an able man, I give him that. But he dislikes a matter that he can't work out in five, ten minutes tops. He'll mount a decent manhunt if he's clear on who he's looking for, or round up any Mexicans who might be handy if he's not. On this deal, though...I'd have to say he's let us down."

"I'll go out on a limb and say he blames wild animals."

Brisbin nodded. "And he'd be right, in other circumstances. It's the loss of blood that has me stumped, and Sheriff Charley doesn't want to hear about it. Well, the blood and certain other things."

Gideon frowned. "Such as?"

"The last fella we lost was Simon Cain, who lived a few miles north of town, out past the main Bear Valley mines. No family that anybody local knows about. A couple weeks ago, he turned up dead, along with all his cattle, thirty head of 'em. Something or someone got them in the barn, after he'd turned in for the night. I know that much because Cain died in just his union suit and boots, not what he would've worn while he was working. Plus, his steers all died inside their stalls, barned up for overnight."

"And what about the barn?" Thorn asked.

Cain kept the doors barred after dark, from the outside. The backdoors were secured when I got out there, once a neighbor happened by and found the mess. The front was open wide enough to let him in, three feet or so, like something brought him out from sleeping in the house."

"Unarmed?"

"Now, that's another thing. He had an eight-gauge Greener with him."

"That's a lot of gun," Thorn said.

"You bet. And he let off both barrels, too. From where the pellets hit the barn's ceiling, it seemed like he was shooting toward the hayloft."

"And?"

"And nothing," Brisbin said. "Me and my part-time deputy went over every inch up there, but found nary a drop of blood, no skin or fur, damn sure no bodies waiting for us. All the dead were down below. But still..."

"You want to say it," Thorn urged him.

"Up in the loft we found some kinda *drag* marks, what you might expect from hauling bales of hay around, but these plowed *through* the scattered bits of straw. And on the wood up there, I could've sworn there was something like claw marks."

"Claws suggest an animal," Thorn said, remembering a

time, two years ago, when claw marks hadn't meant an animal at all. Not even close,

"You'd think that," Brisbin said. "And there was some mess that we smelled up there, like something with a kidney problem took a piss amongst the hay bales."

"Is there any way a bear or cougar could've gotten up into the loft?" Thorn asked.

"I'll say no to the bear, since one the size it took to slaughter Cain and thirty steers would be too heavy for the wooden ladder going up there. I supposed a cougar *might* have made it, if it felt like climbing fifteen feet straight up, but get this: there were no claw marks on any rungs or railings of the ladder. Then, I have to ask *why* a big cat would even try that climb, with thirty dead steers waiting to be eaten down below."

"It might have heard Cain coming from the house."

"Granted, but wouldn't it just wait and jump him when he came inside? And come to that, *how* would a cougar even get inside a locked-up barn? We found no scratches anywhere outside, like something clawing at the doors or climbing up to reach the open loft that way, around in back."

"You've got a point."

"Then, there's the matter of the wounds, not just at Cain's place, but the other ranch I mentioned, and the mine watchman. Whatever killed those folks, and animals on other spreads, *ripped* into necks and shoulders, leaving ragged open wounds, without eating the flesh. And where's the goddamn blood?"

"There is a kind of bat that lives on blood, native to South America."

"And Mexico. You bet. I saw one two, three years ago, last time a carnival passed through. The fella had it in a cage, under a blanket, and he fed it pig's blood, fifteen cents a peek from fools like me to watch it eat. Ugly as sin, it was. Thing is—"

"I know," Thorn said. "They're relatively small."

"The one I saw was mouse-size, maybe three inches from snout to tail. You could've dunked it in a teacup. If it weighed a full two ounces, I'd have been surprised."

"And what about the bites you've seen since this all started?"

"Measured some of 'em and wrote it down. On average, they measured seven inches wide and packed a bunch of teeth. There wasn't anything dainty about it, like the bat I saw caged up. That one lapped blood out of a dish, just like a cat with milk."

"And what about the scratches in the hayloft," Gideon inquired, "or any other signs."

"The marks up in the hayloft *could* have been a cougar, but that brings us back to how it got inside the barn, how and why it climbed a ladder, all of that."

"No marks around the bodies, animal or human, other than the bites?"

"Oh, there were marks, all right," said Brisbin. "Simon Cain was clean enough, as desert ranchers go, but sweeping dust out of the barn must not have preyed much on his mind. We found marks on the floor where he'd been thrashing when he died, and something else. It almost looked like..."

"What?"

"Sounds stupid, but it almost looked like someone flung a tarpaulin on top of him, from up there in the loft. That can't be right, though. He'd have hit the other fellow with his Greener, and there wasn't a tarpaulin on the ranch, much less inside the barn."

"Something to think about," Thorn said, part of his mind already working on the riddle. "What about the other bodies."

"Some of the livestock had claw marks on 'em. Sheriff Charley took that as the only proof he needed for a cougar or a bear being involved."

"Makes sense I guess, up to a point."

"And something else, about the bears. We've got no shortage of 'em, but they mostly hibernate between October or November and the early part of March. That means our raider, if it *was* a bear, skipped denning up this winter and kept hunting straight on through, living on blood alone instead of meat."

"Cougars don't hibernate," Thorn said.

"No Sir, they don't. The sheriff noted that to me, as well. It still leaves all the main objections to a cat being behind these kills."

"So, what have you been thinking?"

"Honestly? I haven't got a damned idea. I thought of rustlers, but they'd make off with the stock, instead of killing it and leaving it for scavengers. Same thing applies to redskins coming off the rez or up from Mexico. They'd either steal the animals or butcher them and take away the meat. As for the dead folks, hell, I'm stumped."

"Tell me about the other three."

"Well, Ernie Givens was the first to go. He spent his nights at the Elvira mine, a little shack out there, and likely slept more than he watched the property. One morning, two days after Christmas, when the foreman and his people went to work at dawn, they found Ernie a couple yards inside the mine shaft with his throat ripped out like I've been telling you, pale as a ghost from loss of blood."

"What about signs around the body?"

"Couldn't say. The miners work twelve hours a day, past dusk in fall and winter, not that they can tell the difference underground. The shaft is mostly stone, smoothed out by boots and wagons bringing up the ore. Elvira's mostly silver, but the owner—Phil Rutter, lives up in Tucson—keeps on hoping they'll strike gold."

"No doubt you checked to see if the watchman had any enemies."

"I did that, for a fact. Came up with nothing but a wrangle back in June, between him and another fella when one of the flossies at the Gold Dust double-booked an hour of her time. The other guy left town in August and nobody's seen him since."

"Nothing to kill over?"

"I wouldn't think so, once he sobered up. And not how it was done, unless he had a screaming crazy streak nobody noticed."

"And the other two? The man and wife?"

"Homer and Elsie Farnum, down here from a spread that went bust on them in Nevada, two years back. They hoped to make a go of it this time—who doesn't?—and had put the word around that they were looking forward to a family."

"Same circumstances as the other killings?" Gideon inquired.

"Not carbon-copy, but the bite marks all looked pretty much the same. Different sizes, but they weren't that far apart in measurement. The way I worked it out, Homer was taken down when he got up from supper, left some of it on the table and went out to check his stock. We're talking sheep in a corral this time. Best guess, Elsie went out to find him when he didn't come back straight away. We found her near the barn, but not inside. Homer was in the pen with thirty-one dead sheep, all of 'em bitten, barely any blood around."

"No point in asking about enemies, I guess?"

"I talked to damn near everyone in town," said Brisbin. "Everyone who claimed to know the Farnums, anyhow. Nobody had a beef with 'em, or else wouldn't fess up to it. I even tried to think of someone who'd have trailed them down here from Nevada, but for what? To gnaw their throats and do the same thing to a flock of sheep? Besides, if there's a man or men out there with mouths that made these wounds, somebody needs to shoot 'em first and skip the questions afterward."

"Okay. I'd say you're dealing with a mystery."

"Thank you for that." Brisbin sounded relieved. "And can you help us with it?"

"I can't promise anything ahead of time," Thorn said. "Some jobs pan out and others don't. I've lost a few. On balance, though, I've solved more than I've walked away from."

Brisbin nodded. Said, "I couldn't ask for anything beyond your best effort. Hell, I've already failed."

"Not necessarily. These things take time. I know that's hard to hear, with people dying, but it's true."

"Uh-huh. Same thing with any other crime."

"Except that if you're dealing with an animal, it might not be a crime, per se. The deaths are homicides, or course, but animals don't know a thing about the law. They live by instinct: feed, mate, sleep, repeat."

"I couldn't say which scares me more," Brisbin allowed. "A crazy man or *men*, on one hand; on the other, some cold-blooded *thing*."

"You understand that man or animal, there could be killing at the end of this."

"Show me the brute or beast responsible, and I'll be first in line to put 'em down."

"All right." Thorn glanced out through the marshal's window, where full dusk had fallen on Montana Camp. "Tomorrow, after breakfast, I should take a look around the places where it happened, starting with the last one first."

"I'll take you out, no problem. Leave my deputy in charge of town till we get back. One thing we haven't talked about..."

"Which is?"

"The article I read about you didn't say how much you charge, a deal like this."

Thorn smiled. "I normally don't ask for any compensation. Now and then—if I work for a company, let's say—they'll put a little something in the pot. If someone's offered a reward for the solution of a case and I can close it, then I split the money with whoever's helped me out. Rest of the time, I like to think of it as...personal enlightenment."

"You're saying free?"

"I mostly pay my own way in the world."

"Well, hell, a body can't ask any more than that."

"Bearing in mind there can't be any guarantees," Thorn said. "I haven't got a crystal ball or anything like that."

"Right now, I'd settle for an educated guess. Until tomorrow morning, then?"

"Tomorrow morning," Thorn agreed.

Both men rose from their chairs, shook hands again, and Gideon went back to his hotel.

THREE

MARCH 3, 1877

Breakfast at the Mother Lode was two fried eggs, bacon *and* ham, with cut-up fried potatoes on the side and some kind of thick toast done up just right. Thorn had a different waitress, figuring that Freckles worked a later shift, but she was just as quick with coffee refills, so he left another dollar tip and caught a smile as he was headed out the door, down toward the livery.

Lute Brisbin met him halfway there, accompanied by a thick-bodied deputy whose eyes came up around Thorn's shoulder, though the ten-gallon hat he wore made him appear taller. His name was Winfield Cowan, but he went by "Win." Based on his steady frown, Gideon guessed it was a simple shortening and not an omen of his outlook on the world—especially not these days, with the shadow that was lingering over Montana Camp.

The good things about Cowan, at first meeting, were his firm handshake and seeming comfort with the Colt Open Top revolver on his hip. He wore it on the left but shook hands with his right, in deference to common practice, but Thorn didn't know if that meant he was ambidextrous.

Never mind.

After the introduction, Brisbin said, "Before we ride out to the Cain place, I was thinking you should meet Doc Wyman. He's our sawbones, patches folk up hereabouts. They need a hospital, the nearest one's in Phoenix, if you want to call it that, which as you may know is one hundred eighty miles northwest. Nobody I know of who's tried it ever made it there alive."

"Nobody," Win Cowan agreed.

"Besides, Doc Wyman made a study of the dead—dead *people,* anyhow, he's not a vet—before Gus Mullins puts 'em in the ground."

"Mullins would be your undertaker," Thorn surmised.

"The one and only," Brisbin said.

Dr. Wyman's office sat between an alley and a dry goods store. A bell over the street entrance jangled when Marshal Brisbin led the way inside, the doctor coming out of a backroom to meet his morning callers before Win Cowan could close the door behind him. Tall and lean, with thinning sandy hair and a mustache to match, the doctor—Herschel Wyman, as he introduced himself—wore wire-rimmed spectacles that seemed intent on sliding down his nose, so that he pushed them up using his middle finger, like he didn't know the gesture was considered rude.

Lute Brisbin introduced Thorn to the doctor and they shook on it. To fill the momentary silence, Gideon observed, "You work on Saturdays."

"All seven days, sometimes," Wyman replied. "It's hit-and-miss, most of my patients coming from the mines. Besides, I live upstairs, so people come whatever time they feel the need."

The marshal cleared his throat before he said, "I'm getting help from Mr. Thorn about the killings, Doc."

"So, nothing from the county seat," Wyman replied.

"Sheriff Shibell has more important things to do," said Brisbin.

"Ah. I can't help hoping that his diligence or lack of it will be remembered at election time."

"I guess we'll see."

The doctor turned to Gideon. "So you're some kind of expert on peculiar deaths?"

"I've seen a few," Thorn said, not feeling any need to be specific.

"If you could describe the injuries, Doc, I'd appreciate it."

"I don't see a problem there," Wyman replied. "No confidentiality between a doctor and the dead."

"You dealt with all four victims?" Gideon inquired.

"Three of them when they were still alive, and all four after," Wyman said. "Homer and Elsie Farnum came in twice, with minor ailments. Garth Jordan was the watchman, and I'd only seen him once before, to splint a broken finger. Simon Cain, I never met."

"And would you say the circumstances of their deaths were similar?"

"Damned near identical," said Wyman. "There were small discrepancies, of course. Three of the four had throat wounds, deep enough for teeth to mark the vertebrae, but Elsie Farnum's was a bit off-target from the others, mainly on her shoulder, about here."

The doctor clapped a hand over his left shoulder, just where it joined the throat.

"And the bite sizes, Doctor?"

"I measured all of them, for both circumference and

diameter. It's not precise, you understand, with torn flesh and passage of time after the injury, dead tissue shrinking back some."

"Your best estimates are all I need," Thorn said.

"I'd say the bites on Garth and Mr. Cain were nigh on to identical. Each one was six inches across, as near as I could make it, and about nine inches in circumference."

"The other two?"

"Both smaller, but neither the same. The wound on Homer was about five inches wide, seven around. Elsie's was smaller still. Call the diameter four and a half inches, and maybe six for the circumference."

"No other bites on any of the victims?"

"None except the ones that killed them."

"And any other injuries that you took note of?"

Wyman nodded, pushed his glasses up. "With Mr. Cain, I found four broken ribs, two on each side of the sternum, which is—"

"The breastbone," Thorn finished his thought.

"Exactly. It appeared that something fairly heavy must've landed on his chest while he was lying down, before...the rest of it."

Thorn turned to Marshal Brisbin. "And you said there wasn't anything on top of him or nearby, in the barn?"

"Nothing except those marks in dust I mentioned, like somebody dropped a tarpaulin that wasn't there."

Returning his attention to the doctor, Gideon inquired, "And did the other three have any injuries besides the fatal bites?"

"Scratches and bruises, likely caused by scuffling with whatever killed them. Oh, and Elsie Farnum's right shoulder was dislocated from its socket. I surmise she raised that arm to shield her face or throat and took a solid hit that brought her down."

"So, impact from whatever killed her, then."

"Undoubtedly. I can't hazard an estimate of weight, but I can tell you that it wasn't human. No one that I've ever heard of on the planet has a mouth like that, much less a set of jagged teeth between a half-inch and three-quarters long."

"No chance at all?"

"I'd say it was impossible," Wyman replied. "The average human mouth is no more than three inches wide, and even gaping open, the circumference wouldn't exceed five inches in a good-sized man. Beyond that, bony structure of the jaw and skull would have to grow out of proportion to the point your killer couldn't step outside without folks spotting him and calling him a freak. And there's the other thing."

"Which is?"

"Based on my measurements, there must be three of them, at least. That means they breed. Try to imagine how a family of freaks like that could pass unnoticed in the world, particularly when they leave a trail of mutilated bodies in their wake."

Thorn saw the sense of that. "I take it then," he said, "you've never heard of anything like this before."

"Never," said Wyman. "And I hope to God I never do again."

Shadow was glad to be out of his stall and saddled up, after Thorn took some time communing silently with Belle. The mule was bored, which seemed to be its normal state, but wasn't out of sorts in any way Thorn could detect.

Lute Brisbin's mount, another tenant of the stable, was a mouse dun gelding that, like Shadow, seemed appreciative of a chance to stretch its legs. Brisbin had stopped off at his office, on their walk down to the livery, and snagged a Winchester, one of the "Yellow Boys" debuted in 1866, nicknamed for its receiver fashioned from a bronze/brass alloy. It fired .44 rimfire Henry cartridges, with sixteen packed into its magazine and maybe one more up the spout if Lute thought he was riding into danger.

Which, Gideon thought, could be a fair assumption in this case.

Doc Wyman had been adamant about their quarry being some kind of an animal—and more than one, in fact. Gideon thought back to the job he'd tackled in New Mexico, two years ago this summer, wherein a demented killer had devised a sort of killing costume from the skull and claws of a large grizzly, wearing those accoutrements to maul his human prey. He wasn't likely to forget that waking nightmare, but the fiend he'd finally put down hadn't been capable of altering his lethal headdress, changing it in size or shape.

So, the thing stalking Montana Flats wasn't a man. Which left...what?

That was where Thorn had to rein in his imagination, looking back on all the eerie things he'd faced since he began his sojourn in the West. The problem with imagination, as he'd learned, was that it might either inflate or minimize a peril. Even when his life wasn't at risk, as in the case of his relationship with Dinah Pilcher, Thorn could still be taken by surprise if he let down his guard.

And that kind of mistake, in his world, could be fatal, more often than not.

Riding along Bear Valley, north from town, they passed by several working mines, a couple of the foremen waving at the marshal if they noticed him. Each mine was labeled with a sign, all bearing women's names for some reason: Lucinda, Ruby, Annabelle, Elvira.

Passing that one, Thorn asked Lute, "Is that Garth Jordan's shack out front?"

"It was. Office by day, and lookout post by night. They've got a new watchman since Garth was killed. I haven't met him. S'posed to be some kind of shooter down from Kansas City."

"Not a big-game hunter?"

"Not unless you count big game as some guy on a WANTED poster, with a target on his back and price tag on his head. Some kind of bounty hunter, way I heard it. Calls himself Jeb Lockhart."

"Never heard of him."

"You haven't missed much," Brisbin said. "You need to see him later, for whatever reason, I can set it up."

Approaching Simon Cain's spread, Thorn picked out a burnt meat odor, as if some incompetent had botched a massive barbecue. He sniffed the breeze and made a sour face.

"I know," said Brisbin, picking up on it. "We could've saved some of the meat, I guess, but no one wanted any part of it, thinking whatever killed the steers might have some kinda taint attached to it. Burnt 'em instead."

"And did it?" Gideon inquired.

"The doc says no, but with a deal like this nobody's ever seen or heard of, how's he really know?"

Good question, Thorn mused. But unless the killer was

some kind of rabid animal—no, make that three or four, at least—he couldn't think what else they might be carrying.

Even without its smell, the ranch had that dead and abandoned feeling he'd experienced before, at other rural killing sites between Missouri and the West Coast, down from Canada to Mexico. Not haunted—he had felt that, too—but just a place where tragedy had stopped off long enough to reap some souls and then moved on.

But going where?

A solitary vulture watched them from the barn's peaked roof, then lifted off as they drew nearer, flapping up and up to catch a desert thermal for another looping ride in search of food.

Thorn didn't try to touch it with his mind. For some reason he didn't grasp, birds of all kinds appeared resistant to what Gideon regarded as his special talent. He was shy of giving it a fancy name, although he'd heard someone back east was calling it "telepathy."

Why bother naming it, as long as it came through for him most times?

They rode into the farmyard side by side, dismounting next to an empty corral. Brisbin tied off his gelding's reins to a fence rail, while Thorn let Shadow wander as he pleased.

"Not worried something hereabouts might spook him?" asked the lawman.

"Not much."

"Well, you know your animal, I guess. Care for a look inside the house?"

"Did anything happen in there?"

The marshal shook his head. "Nothing, as far as I could tell. Checked out the place, o'course. Cain wasn't much of a housekeeper, living on his own, but there was nothing out of place like it was ransacked. No one left to kill in there, once Cain went down, and that was in the barn."

"Let's try that, then."

Cain left his rifle in its saddle boot, but Brisbin took his Yellow Boy before they moved on to the silent barn. Gideon reckoned that if they met something his twin Colts couldn't stop, a rifle wouldn't be much use to him.

"The door was like this when you found it?" he asked Brisbin, meaning open wide enough for someone roughly his size to intrude.

"Just like that, yeah."

"And all the steers are gone now?"

"Chickens, too. Since they weren't hurt, his neighbors to the north, the Kubitchevs, asked whether they could take 'em. Saw no harm in it, so off they went."

"Chickens won't help us," Thorn agreed. And even if they'd stayed behind, he couldn't have communicated with them, learning what—if anything—they'd seen or heard the night that Death dropped by.

"The Kubitchevs are Polish?" Thorn asked.

"Russian. Does it matter?"

"Doubtful."

"Here goes, then."

Brisbin was first into the barn, Thorn on his heels. Inside, there was a smell of old, dried blood and something else Thorn had to stop and puzzle over.

"Did the rancher wet himself?"

Brisbin blinked at him from the shadows. Answered, "That's some nose you've got. I guess you know folks do that, lose control downstairs when something kills 'em."

"Right."

Thorn didn't have to ask where Cain had fallen. While the dust around the spot had been disturbed by boots—

most likely Brisbin and the others who had found Cain, carting him back to Montana Camp—a splash of old blood on the floor still made the story clear.

A splash, but not much more.

Your average-sized person held about eleven pints, and Thorn guessed that a cup or less had spilt from Simon Cain, as if whatever killed him was a trifle sloppy when it fed.

"And there were steers in all the stalls?" he asked Brisbin.

"Full up. All killed the same as Simon. You can see the bloodstains."

He was right. Since steers were larger, big hearts pumping more blood through their arteries and veins, most of the stains displayed on beds of straw were relatively larger than the dead man's, and the straw had been disturbed by thrashing hooves, each beast in line watching its fellows die before its turn arrived. They'd voided bowels and bladders in their panic, just the same as any other animal.

"Okay," Thorn said. "I can't tell much from this, except it doesn't seem the steers were all attacked at once. Some of them had a chance to watch and worry while the bloodletting went on."

"So, not some kind of gang, then," said the marshal.

"You heard what Doc Wyman said about the mouths and teeth. No men did this, although..."

"Though what?" Lute prodded him.

"You couldn't tell if there were any human tracks beside the victim's when you got here?"

"Cain's, a couple from the neighbor who looked in and found the mess." A pause, and then he asked, "Hey, are you thinking some bastard came in and watched this going on?"

"I wouldn't say that."

"Because if he did, I've got a lunatic running around. If there was more than one of 'em, God help us."

Lunatic, Thorn thought, and had to ask. "Was there a correlation you could see between attacks and phases of the moon?"

"Not even close."

"Okay. I ought to have a look up in the loft."

"Your show. Go on ahead."

Thorn scrambled up the wooden ladder, heaved himself into the loft and scanned it, grateful for the sunlight streaming through its open hay door. There were ten to fifteen bales stacked up, no sign they'd been disturbed, but now he smelled what Brisbin had described before, tracing it to a brownish stain soaking into one of the bales. He couldn't judge its volume without probing, calculating, but Thorn guessed the killer—or one of them—had excreted three or four cups of some dark, malodorous liquid, now dried the rusty color of old blood.

And then he saw the scratches on the hayloft's wooden floor, four visible on each side of a drag mark through the dust and bits of hay, with two more widely separated and well forward from the rest. It looked as if some creeping thing had scuttled from the hay bales and then launched itself on top of Simon Cain, crushing him to the floor below.

But what in hell could that have been?

"I've seen enough," he told the marshal from on high, wondering if he'd missed something that would sneak around later and literally bite him in the ass.

"Suits me," Brisbin replied. "This place is giving me the creeps."

FOUR

Brisbin was silent for a time, then spoke up once again when they were passing the Elvira mine, back toward Montana Camp. "No sign of Lockhart yet," he said.

"Maybe some other time."

"Before we get to town, there's someone else I think you ought to meet."

Intrigued, Thorn asked, "Who's that?"

"A foreigner. Well, he lives *here* now, seems to have his roots dug in, but he came down from New York City. Landed there from Germany or Austria, I don't remember which it was, off-hand."

"And I should meet him...why?"

"Well, he's a doctor. Not like Wyman, but one of those whadda-you-call-its. Has a Ph.D."

"So, not a *doctor* doctor."

"Right. Thing is, he works on animals."

"When you say, 'Works on'..."

"I'm not saying this right," Brisbin groused. "He's not a vet, either. Does research at his place, a mile or so out west of town. Studies how critters *evolve*, he says. Is that the word? I say it right?"

"Exactly right."

At Harvard, Thorn had read Charles Darwin's *On the Origin of Species,* published to tremendous controversy just before the Civil War. The jabber was still going on about his theory of evolution via natural selection, with the hide-bound preachers on one side calling it blasphemy against the legend of creation, while some scientific minds had opened far enough to grant that Mother Nature might select some species to survive, adapt, and populate the Earth while others dwindled, fell away, and went extinct.

Thorn had no problem with the theory. It explained why many prehistoric species had died out, not from the flood of Noah, but from changes in their physical environment and climate. The mastodon and woolly mammoth had turned into nearly hairless elephants in Africa and Asia, for example, not because some deity had willed it to be so or mammoths walked too slow in ancient times to get a reservation on the Ark before it sailed.

Conversely, Thorn still had good reason to believe that some species, either unrecognized by modern-day biologists or thought to be extinct, might be hiding somewhere on the planet, maybe even getting up to devilment from time to time.

In fact, he'd met a few of them, himself, and lived to tell the tale—at least, so far.

Some clergymen, he guessed, would never bow to the advance of science, most particularly when it sparked an exodus from Sunday pews and cut into their tax-free offerings. They'd live and die, kicking and screaming that the only science you could trust was the mythology of Genesis, as laid out by themselves.

"What's this guy's name?" Thorn asked.

"Horst Müller," Brisbin said, doing his best to speak with a vaguely Germanic accent. "I most likely messed that up. The way he says it, sounds more like a horse that drives a mule team." After chuckling at his own *bon mot,* the marshal said, "I mostly call him 'Doctor,' let it go at that. Don't see much of him, anyway."

"Not big on towns, then," Thorn surmised.

"Don't know about that," Brisbin said. "Claims he spent five or six years in New York before he came back here. Before that, he was studying or maybe teaching at some big-time European school. Not sure I got all that exactly straight."

"It could be both," Gideon said. "Some scholars pick up their degrees and move straight into research at their *alma maters.*"

"So, long story short, they never get away from school?"

Thorn had to smile at that, before he said, "You hit it on the head."

The buildings of Montana Camp were coming into view now, but the marshal took a dusty side road before reaching the town's wooden sign. Thorn followed him for something like a mile, the town receding to their left-rear, until they could see a large house and outbuildings standing up ahead.

The house was Spanish in design—or Mexican, depending how you looked at it—with sandy-colored stucco covering what Thorn guessed were brick walls, likely adobe. A low wall ran all the way around the place, encompassing the house, a stable, privy, and some sheds. Inside the fenced perimeter stood tall saguaro cactuses in place of trees, with smaller prickly pears and yucca plants bearing white flowers, sometimes known as Spanish bayonets.

Low maintenance, from all that Thorn could see, which would be perfect for a man who didn't care for company, preferring to get lost in books.

But how had anyone from Europe, having pulled up stakes to live in New York City, wound up here?

The stucco wall possessed a gate, but it was standing open when they reached it, whether as an invitation to outsiders or an absent-minded accident, Thorn couldn't guess. His escort didn't hesitate to ride on through it, reigning up before a broad veranda with no furniture in sight. Following Brisbin's lead, Gideon dismounted from Shadow, tying him loosely where he could drink from a rough-hewn water trough. Thorn saw no source of water in the hacienda's front yard, reckoning there had to be a well somewhere around in back.

Before they stepped onto the porch, the tall front door swung open and a slender man of Indio extraction stepped out of the house. Dressed all in white, bareheaded with his blue-black hair cut shoulder length, his age was indeterminate, but from the deep lines in his face, Thorn pegged him somewhere in the range of forty-five to sixty.

"*Hola,* Pablo," the marshal said in greeting. "Might we have a word with *el señor*? Somebody here I think he ought to meet."

"I go see," Pablo answered in a raspy voice, then turned and shut the door behind him as he reentered the house.

"Not big on warmth," Thorn said.

"The doctor likes his privacy, no doubt. Not that standoffish once you get to know him, but I wouldn't count on any invitations to a garden party."

When the door opened again, Pablo was nowhere to be seen. Instead, a portly white man stood before them, wearing gray slacks and a vest to match over a white shirt, long-sleeved, with a braided leather bolo tie whose clasp was jade. A gold-rimmed pince-nez rode his beaklike nose.

"Good afternoon, Marshal." The master's voice was higher-pitched than Thorn would've expected from a man his size, standing six feet or so and weighing upwards of two hundred pounds. "And who is your companion?"

"Doctor, meet Gideon Thorn. He's come to help me with the troubles I've been having."

"Ah. *Die Morde.*"

That was German for "the killings," Thorn knew. Even so, the doctor could be Austrian as easily as German, maybe even Swiss.

Müller shook hands with Thorn—a damp, soft clasp, quickly released—and asked, "Are you some kind of specialist in murder?"

"Killings by an animal wouldn't be treated as a murder," Thorn replied. "They don't know anything about man's law and can't be held accountable in court."

Müller nodded. "*Das ist richtig,* but accountable they shall be, none the less, in human eyes, *ja*? You would kill them, I suppose?"

"I'd want to stop them. Killing isn't always necessary."

"So, a man after my own heart, possibly? But I forget my *manieren,* gentlemen. Please, come inside, out of the sun."

He led the way, with Brisbin on his heels, Thorn bringing up the rear. Pablo stepped out of shadows to their right and shut the door, his sandals silent on the tiled floor.

"To the drawing room, I think," Müller declared. "Pablo, fetch brandy, eh?"

Without waiting to see his order followed, Müller led his guests into a spacious parlor, telling them, "I never understood this name, the 'drawing room.' It clearly has nothing to do with art."

"From what I understand," Thorn said, "it started out as a *with*drawing room, where folks went after dinner with their guests, if they had some. The French call them *levees*."

Müller blinked at him, then broke out in a smile. To Brisbin, he said, "Do you see, Marshal? Today I learn something, always a benefit." And then, to both of them, "Sit, please. Pablo will bring the brandy momentarily."

The furniture ran toward rococo pieces with the wood apparently hand-carved, upholstered in a fading floral chintz. Wherever it had come from, Thorn knew that it wasn't manufactured locally or recently. He sat with Brisbin on a sofa, ample space between them, while their host settled into a wing chair of his own, facing his uninvited visitors across a long, broad coffee table. Pablo reappeared before they had a chance to speak again, depositing three snifters of amber liqueur. Thorn tasted his and found it to be cognac, aged Napoléon.

"Well, thanks for this, Doctor," said Brisbin. "We won't take up too much of your time."

"*Es ist nichs,*" Müller answered him. "As I told you before, if there is any way that I may help you with these...shall we say events, if not murders"—a nod toward Thorn—"then I am pleased to do so."

"Trouble is, I'm still not clear on that part," Brisbin said. "But since Doc Maynard's sure our folks are being killed by animals, not men, I thought that Mr. Thorn should meet you, anyway. You studying all kinds of animals, that is."

"Alas," Müller replied, "not *all* kinds, Marshal. Mr. Thorn, I am by training what we call an evolutionist. If you know what that is—"

"I got a dose of Darwin at Harvard," Thorn interrupted him.

"An educated man! Most excellent." Müller seemed

pleased. "I studied under Dr. Gregor Mendel in Vienna. He, of course, primarily concerns himself with plant hybridization, dominant versus recessive traits which can be singled out and bred for stronger, more abundant crops and what have you. I have applied his work to animals, the lower species. Most of my experiments so far have been on flatworms, with a few on the amphibians in what you might say is the larval stage."

"That anything like pollywogs?" Brisbin inquired.

"The very same, Marshal. A pollywog, or tadpole, is the larval stage of all amphibians, whether they grow to be a frog, a toad, a salamander, any breed at all. Because their transformation from a legless infant—fetal, although hatched from eggs, developing outside the mother's body—can be clearly witnessed, they help us document the proof of evolutionary theory."

"And during the observation, you conduct experiments?" Thorn asked.

"Indeed. My work is still in what I call the stage of infancy itself, but I have hopes for matching Dr. Mendel's feats in time."

"What brings you to the Southwest, Doctor?" Gideon inquired.

"Two things, sir. First, I fear my health is not so *gut*. Some difficulty with my lungs, but stabilized I hope, with your dry climate here. Also, while many fools regard the desert as a vast wasteland, in truth it harbors many unique forms of life, both plant and animal. Are you familiar with *Eulimnadia texana*, for example?"

"Rings a faint bell from my classes in zoology."

"Its common name is desert shrimp. They live for many years as tiny cysts, appearing lifeless, until rain comes, when they spring to life, swiftly maturing in temporary pools and laying eggs that can remain dormant until the next rain, often decades later."

"That doesn't strike me as much of a life," Brisbin chimed in.

"But it is *theirs,* Marshal. The only life they have. *Eulimnadia texana* are sexually dimorphic. That means some are males, their front legs modified as claws for grasping when they feed and mate. Others are hermaphrodites, possessing reproductive organs of both male and female, who can mate with males or fertilize their own eggs, but cannot mate with other hermaphrodites."

"Sounds too confusing for my taste," Brisbin replied. "I like the old man-woman way of doing things."

Müller smiled broadly, sipped his cognac, and replied, "*Ist gut.*" He then lapsed into heavily accented French, adding, "*Vive le difference!*"

Thorn tried to bring their conversation back on point. "Doctor, I'm guessing that you couldn't say what any large man-killing predators around these parts might be, or why nobody's ever heard of them before?"

"Alas, no." Müller's frown was one of disappointment in himself. "As I have said, I only work with small and harmless species, studying growth and transformation in their young. As to a creature or a species that could overpower humans and their livestock, I am sadly *ahnungslos*—clueless, as you would say—and cannot even guess where you should start to look."

Brisbin quaffed the remainder of his cognac, set his empty glass back on the table. "Well, I guess that says it all. Doctor, I want to thank you once again for seeing us, and to apologize for stealing time from your experiments."

"*Nonsens.* My worms and tadpoles will not miss me, and

they have nowhere to go. Feel free to visit anytime. I only wish that I could be of help."

He walked them to the door and out to the veranda, where their horses waited in the shade cast by his house. They shook hands all around—the doctor's grasp no more assertive than the last time—before Thorn and Brisbin mounted up. Riding away, Thorn spotted Pablo coming after them, across the yard, to close the gate.

"Looks like they're shutting down," Thorn said.

"Can't be too careful in these parts," Brisbin replied. "You never know who might come calling."

"But the gate was open when we got here."

"Pablo likely had some chores to do around the place and just forgot it. Anyway, what did you think of Dr. Müller?"

"He reminds me of this one professor, used to be at Harvard. He's retired now, what they call emeritus, and he was born in Delaware, not Germany, but he resembled Müller more or less, got off the track on any subject near and dear to him."

"I'd say that sums the doctor up," Brisbin conceded.

Entering Montana Camp, they passed the Lucky Strike saloon before reaching the livery. A rangy man was coming out just then, wearing a flannel shirt with sleeves rolled to his elbows, denim pants and dusty boots, a slouch hat pulled down low over his eyes against the later afternoon sun. The one outstanding thing about him was his gunbelt: jet-black, hand-tooled leather with a bone-handled Colt Bisley Frontier pistol in a low-slung holster, shiny cartridges gleaming from loops around his narrow hips.

"That's Jeb Lockhart," said Brisbin, voice low-pitched. "He's likely heading out to the Elvira now. Wouldn't believe, to look at him, he's killed more a dozen men or so for money."

Thorn watched as the bounty hunter loosed a buckskin mare from her place at the barroom's hitching post and climbed aboard, flicking a nod toward Brisbin and ignoring Gideon as he rode north along the town's unnamed main street.

"You say he hunts big game, on top of men?"

"Supposedly. I've heard him talk about grizzlies and moose he's shot. When he's been liquidating, he might tell you that he's been to Africa and killed an elephant or some such, but I take that with a grain of salt."

"You never know."

"Guess not. But what I *do* know is he hasn't bagged one of our monsters yet. Of course, he's only been around Montana Camp a couple weeks."

"Maybe he'll bag one yet," Thorn said.

"I'm not holding my breath. The guy owns the Elvira, Phil Rutter, promised him a bonus if he kills whatever did for Garth Jordan, but so far he's only earned his basic salary."

"Milking the job, you think?"

"That's not the way I read him. Lockhart doesn't strike me as a shirker, and I've known a fair number of those. More like he's just biding his time and waiting for a shot."

"With that Colt he was wearing?"

"Likely not. Word has it that he keeps an over-under long gun at the mine, high caliber that takes rifle and shotgun ammunition both. Something like .45-70 Government on top and ten-gauge underneath."

"Maybe he'll have some luck," Thorn said.

"One lucky shot won't do it, if Doc Wyman's right about having a bunch of critters on the loose."

Shadow didn't mind Thorn putting him away, after a brushing to relax him. Thorn and Brisbin parted company outside the stable, planning to meet up again next morning. In the meantime, Thorn was counting on a ride out to the Cain spread, maybe staying overnight at the most recent scene of an attack.

He didn't put much stock in criminals returning to the scene of a prior crime, but dealing with an animal was different. If one found food someplace, it was likely to try the same again, in hopes of getting lucky twice. An eight-gauge hadn't stopped the thing last time, but Thorn would be packing his Winchester for rapid fire, backed up by the big Sharps.

First, though, his growling stomach made its hunger known. After a quick stop at the Copper Queen, checking for messages and finding none, he started for the restaurant he hadn't sampled yet, Delmonico's. Eat first, then sleep a while, before he headed north again, prepared to stay awake all night.

FIVE

Inside the Copper Queen, roughly a dozen diners eyed Thorn as a slim waitress with hair like straw conveyed him to a corner table, well back from the door. She handed him a menu written out on cardboard that had been around a while, showing a stain or two that hadn't quite come clean. From that, Thorn chose a rib eye steak with baked potato, refried beans, and *torta*, which he knew was flatbread popular in Mexico.

Before the feast, which turned out to be plentiful and tasty, Thorn had coffee, which was weaker than the Mother Lode's but adequate, considering he hoped to catch some sleep before his next hike to the livery. Unless he missed his guess, the now-dead Simon Cain should have a coffee pot and grounds somewhere inside the house his killers hadn't bothered to invade.

They'd come for blood, obtained it, and presumably departed as they'd come, leaving few traces of themselves behind.

That was a puzzler, but Thorn let it go while he enjoyed his meal, ignoring other customers inside the restaurant who plainly didn't think he'd catch them shooting glances his way on the sly.

He knew those looks: stranger in town, dressed all in black and amply armed. Montana Camp must get its share of drifters passing through, but with the gruesome slayings added to it, any new face was suspicious, most particularly when the new arrival had a killer's mien about him.

Did they look the same way at Jeb Lockhart, or had they managed to accept him as a fixture now, replacing one of their lost citizens? Thorn didn't know and didn't care. If strangers chose to judge him at a glance, so be it. Once his job was done—*if* it got done—they'd see the back of him and soon forget that he was ever in their midst.

Back at the Copper Queen, Thorn clomped upstairs, the clerk nowhere in evidence, and let himself into his room. Nothing had been disturbed during his absence, and he kicked his boots off, shed his gunbelt, leaving it beside him as he lay down fully dressed atop his bed's thin floral quilt.

Sleep found him soon enough, roughly four hours worth, and it was dark outside when Thorn's internal clock woke him, approaching half-past seven by his pocket watch. This time, he took both long guns with him when he left his room and went down to the lobby.

While he'd slept, the clerk had reappeared and felt obliged to ask him, "Going hunting, Mister?"

"That's a thought," Gideon told him and stepped into the night.

The hostler was awake and on the job when Thorn entered the livery, asking no questions as to why a man stocked up on guns was heading out after sunset. The way things had been going in Montana Camp, Thorn guessed firearms and furtive movements had become routine.

A light was showing from the marshal's office as he

passed it, Brisbin's deputy seated behind the desk in there, reading a newspaper. Thorn couldn't see enough of him to guess if Win Cowan was nervous over night descending, or if he'd accepted that the killers hadn't struck in town so far and likely wouldn't.

But if they were animals of some kind, would that hold?

The mines that had been going full-blast on his first ride north were silent now, dark for the most part, though Jeb Lockhart had a lamp lit in his shack outside of the Elvira's shaft. Thorn didn't glimpse the man inside or near about, but left him to his work or sleep, whichever took priority.

At last, he reached the Cain spread, rode a circuit of the house and barn before dismounting, leaving Shadow on his own with calming thoughts, not tying up his reins in case something should happen and the stallion had to fight or flee before Thorn came to help him.

At the moment, he judged nothing was impossible, and standing on the porch, a rifle in each hand, Gideon closed his eyes and took a mental reading on the desert night. He lightly touched a prowling coyote, some distance off, and a young rabbit that might end up being supper if it wasn't careful. Nothing else right now, although he knew this kind of country featured a variety of wildlife, much of it nocturnal in the face of days that baked the land.

Inside the house, door shut against the night but left unlatched, Thorn found that he was right about the coffee situation. Simon Cain hadn't been fastidious at cleaning out the percolator, but the water would be boiling anyway. The coffee grounds were in an airtight can—no bugs allowed—and smelled nigh on to fresh when Thorn unscrewed its lid.

He found a stack of cut wood near the stove and got a

fire going, put on the coffee pot, and started on a visual inspection of his weapons. All of them were loaded and well oiled, but checking over them before a shooting, if there was to be one, had become an ingrained habit on Thorn's travels through the West. Something could always go awry, despite his loving care for steel and ammunition, but since there was no guarding against a rare misfire, Gideon concentrated on mechanics, confident that he could usually hit whatever he was aiming at.

What would that be?

Most likely nothing, he acknowledged to himself, but this was logical step one in setting out to hunt whatever had been winnowing the population of Montana Camp. No hits in town so far, which told him that the predators were shy of lights and crowds, but what on Earth *were* they?

The "on Earth" caught him for a second. In his wanderings, he'd seen some things that, strictly speaking, hinted strongly at an afterlife or realm outside the bounds of what most people took for granted as conventional reality. He'd dealt with ghosts and rituals that summoned forces from somewhere *outside,* whatever that might mean. Some of the entities he'd faced would leave straitlaced religious folk shaking their heads in wonder or, more likely, making up their minds to simply not believe.

Which wouldn't help them, as he knew too well, if something from *beyond* reached out to touch or end their puny lives.

A more important matter: would Thorn's weapons be of any use to him, should he meet up with the voracious predators who'd marked Montana Camp as their domain? One of the things had plied its excretory functions in the barn a few yards from the kitchen table where Thorn sat. That, with the victims' wounds and loss of blood, told

Gideon he wasn't dealing with a shade or spirit, but with something physical.

If it peed between meals, smart money said that it would likely bleed if injured.

And if it could bleed, it could be killed someway, somehow.

Sipping a dead man's strong black coffee, playing out his first hand in what Thorn knew might become a waiting game, he could only hope his mobile arsenal—the Sharps, the Winchester, his Colts—would be enough to do the job. If it came down to fighting hand-to-hand, Thorn guessed his muscles and his Bowie might be overmatched.

In which case, he was dead.

THE ELVIRA MINE

Jeb Lockhart was a patient man. Not so much dealing with people face-to-face, in what they chose to call polite society —which, in his personal experience was rarely that polite or welcoming to strangers passing through.

He'd never been much of a Bible-reader, though his folks had tried beating it into him before he'd had enough and hit the trail. Still, Jeb recalled a verse or two, and one of them that stuck with him over the years was Hebrews 13:2, which read, "Be not forgetful to entertain strangers: for thereby some have entertained angels unawares."

Lockhart personally doubted there were any angels—though he'd seen his share of devils, right enough—but he could only laugh at so-called Christians and their attitude toward new acquaintances, so far from welcoming that it was pitiful.

Jeb, for his part, treated strangers in one of three ways, depending on the given situation. Most folks, he was happy to ignore. The ones who offered services he needed, Lockhart treated civilly enough, but wouldn't bow and scrape. As for the ones with prices on their heads and targets on their backs, he put them down without a second thought and sought the nearest handy lawman to collect his cash reward.

And in his spare time, just for fun, he hunted damned near anything that moved.

Tonight, while he was being paid to safeguard the Elvira mine, Jeb had a second job going. There was at least a chance, he thought, that whatever had killed the mine's last watchman might return with easy pickings on its mind.

He hoped so, anyway. Lockhart preferred lying in wait for things he meant to kill, letting them come to him, instead of chasing them around, not knowing when they'd turn on him and take him out.

The marshal in Montana Camp was confident the prowler was some kind of animal, not human, its species unknown and wide open to speculation. Obviously, it was large enough to overpower grown men and their livestock, seemingly without incurring any injury itself.

I'll fix that, Lockhart thought, while sitting in his guard shack, seeing to his main weapon. It was a stout Holland & Holland, custom-made in London, and had cost the better part of Lockhart's bounty from a child killer and rapist whom he'd bagged in Texas sometime back. The bastard hadn't seen it coming, but he definitely *had* it coming, and the Angelina County sheriff who'd been looking for him didn't mind buying a corpse, which spared Lufkin's good people paying for a trial and wasting rope.

Jeb's weapon was a work of art, well worth its price.

He'd let the local lawman, Marshal Brisbin, look it over without handling it, feasting his eyes and seeming envious. The gun's top barrel, rifled, had been chambered for .45-70 Government rounds, each packed with seventy grains of black powder and lead bullets weighing seven-tenths of an ounce. Each left the muzzle at 1,597 feet per second—better than eighteen miles a minute if Lockhart could see that far —and its tang sight was calibrated out to 1,500 yards. For closer work, the Holland's lower ten-gauge barrel handled shotgun shells ranging from birdshot up to quadruple-aught buckshot, each pellet weighing 5.6 ounces. In a pinch, the lower barrel also fired solid slugs, equivalent to a .79-caliber bullet, that would finish off anything the .45-70 didn't knock down.

If all else failed, Lockhart still had his Colt Bisley revolver, packing six .45 rounds. So far, he'd never met a man or animal he couldn't kill with all that firepower at hand.

But first, of course, Jeb had to actually *see* his target, take its measure, and decide which load was better for the job. As usual, he guessed the marshal and Montana Camp's other inhabitants wanted their adversary dead. Once Lockhart had accomplished that and pocketed his pay from Mr. Rutter up in Tucson, Lockhart didn't care whether the beast was buried, barbecued, or stuffed and put in a museum.

If it were the latter, though, he'd have to stick around and make damn sure they spelled his name right on the plaque.

Lockhart was working on his second piping cup of coffee when he heard a noise he didn't recognize outside. Not boots crunching on sand or gravel. Not the patter of coyote paws, nor scuttling of a rodent. Not the slither of a serpent or short-legged Gila monster. It was more like flapping wings, too large for any owl he knew of, while the larger desert raptors would be tucked up in their aeries.

"Better check that out," Jeb muttered, talking to himself.

He took the Holland with him, freed his holster's hammer thong, and left the shack. Outside, a waxing gibbous moon cast faint light over open ground and mine carts, no sign of a prowler on the premises. Lockhart stood barely breathing, waiting for his eyesight to adjust after the lamplight in his guard shack, eyes raised toward the sky where he would logically expect a bird of any kind to be found circling.

Nothing.

He muttered a curse, was just about to give it up, when something passed across the moon, a flicker, there and gone in less time than it took to register on Lockhart's brain. And then he heard the eerie sound again: *whop-whop*, and what else could it be but wings, albeit larger ones than he had ever seen or dreamed.

He cocked both hammers on his H & H, raising the buttstock to his shoulder while he scanned the star field overhead. It made him slightly dizzy, so he braced his feet apart for more stability, keep his death grip on the gun.

Was he imagining the passage of some dark shape overhead? Its movement was erratic, like a spastic painter's brush daubing the stars out with black paint, except they reappeared at once, not lost at all, but only momentarily obscured.

And then, more frightful than the flapping sound, a high-pitched keening pierced his ears, making him flinch. If it had been a smaller sound, Jeb thought he should have recognized it, but he couldn't place it at the moment, either as to where he'd heard it previously, or what caused the noise.

"Goddamn it!"

Lockhart loathed the shiver that ran down his back, even with no one there to see his shoulders hunch with sudden fear, a man preparing to receive a swift, harsh blow.

It came on from behind him, something like an animated canvas flapping to envelop him, talons of some kind ripping into Lockhart's shoulders. Driven to his knees, he lashed out with his long gun, struck something that *grunted,* then let out another squeal and sent him sprawling, while it whirled away and upward into darkness.

Struggling to his knees once more, he shouted at the hungry night, "Come on, you bastard! Show yourself!"

But when it did, the truth of it stunned Lockhart, made him waste his first shot, the .45-70 slug flying high and wide. The Holland's kick against his shoulder almost put Jeb over on his back.

How had he missed something so big?

And Christ, now it was coming back, no more afraid of him than if he were a stripling with a popgun in his hands. Jeb couldn't seem to fire the ten-gauge, realized too late his index finger was outside the Holland's trigger guard, and by the time he had corrected that, his death plowed into him and rode him down, his bent knees cracking painfully, although he scarcely noticed that.

The onslaught felt like being smothered in a blanket while he took a beating. Lockhart felt one of his ribs crack, arms pinned, but he had his finger on the Holland's shotgun now and nearly cackled with relief. Up close, he'd seen the ten-gauge nearly rip a man in two, imagining its catastrophic impact with the muzzle pressed against his would-be killer's flesh.

And then reality wiped out imagination. In his daze, Jeb didn't realize the Holland was pressed down along his squirming right leg, angling toward his foot. The point-blank blast blew off the toe-end of his boot and everything inside it, spewing blood and gristle from his mutilated foot.

He screamed at that and kept on screaming as a snarling mouth clamped at the juncture of his jaw and throat, a bristling set of teeth like daggers shearing through his jawbone, muscle, tendons, severing the jugular and his carotid artery. Lockhart could feel blood gushing out of him, but little of it spilled to soak his shirt. The mouth attached to him was sucking like a plunger, draining him of life while something long and raspy wriggled in the gaping wound.

Jeb tried to reach his Colt, a dying impulse that went nowhere as he felt his heart begin to stutter in his heaving chest. It couldn't pump blood fast enough, but whatever had pinned him to the ground was helping out with that.

It smelled like—what? A dog? Maybe a rat larger than any ever seen on Earth?

And Christ, where did it get so many teeth?

SIX

MARCH 4, 1877

After a long and uneventful night, Thorn rode back to Montana Camp at dawn's first light, checked Shadow back into the livery and spent a little time with Belle, then dropped his rifles at the Copper Queen before he crossed the street for breakfast at the Mother Lode. They must've had a waitress surplus, since he didn't recognize the young woman who seated him, but he picked out a couple of familiar faces at adjacent tables. None of them appeared to recognize him, which was fine with Gideon.

This Sunday morning's breakfast special was a Spanish omelet served up with a chicken enchilada and a heap of tangy rice. Thorn was mopping the final remnants from his plate with a half-biscuit when the street door opened and he spotted Marshal Brisbin checking out the restaurant, making a beeline for his table.

"Tried the hotel first," said Brisbin, sounding out of breath. "Clerk said you stayed out overnight, then came in here."

Thorn frowned. Answered, "I'm glad it's only you he told, or else I'd need to have a word with him about discretion."

Sitting down across from Gideon, the lawman asked, "You wanna tell me where you went?"

"Wasted my time out at the Cain place," Thorn replied, "hoping his killer might swing back around to grab another meal."

"It doubled back, all right," said Brisbin, scowling. "But it went to the Elvira mine."

"From your expression, I'm guessing that Lockhart didn't bag it."

"Right you are, but *it* bagged *him*. One of the early morning crew found what was left of him and rode back into town. Got hold of me after he'd stopped off at the Dry Gulch for a couple shots of rye. Supposed to calm him down, I guess, but he was babbling like he'd lost his mind. Might have, for all I know. Doc Wyman was giving him some kind of potion for his nerves."

Sedated before Thorn could speak to him. That wouldn't help.

"What did he say, Marshal?"

"Long story short, he rode out before sunrise. Mines around here run on Sundays, same as any other day. So, it was still dark when he got there, Ezra says—his name is Ezra Butterfield—and he was just in time to see some 'big black thing' flapping away on wings he could've wrapped around his horse. Now, understand, Ezra's been known to pull a cork, and not just when he's had a shock like this, either."

"Go on with what he said."

"Right. Once this thing flew off, if it was ever there at

all, he spots Jeb Lockhart stretched out on the ground. Torn up the way he was—his throat just like the others, maybe something with his foot that Ezra couldn't quite make out in the excitement—Jeb was obviously dead as Pharaoh. Ezra wheeled around and rode back here to spread the news. O' course, he had to stop and wet his whistle, first."

"What's your next move?" Thorn asked.

"I sent Win Cowan out to baby-sit the stiff and make sure no one fiddles with it. Next, I need to round up anyone who's coming with me. That would be Doc Wyman, Gus Mullins, and likely his apprentice, eighteen-year-old kid who wants to be an undertaker for some reason, name's Othaniel Morley."

"Count me in," Thorn said.

"Was hoping you'd say that."

"I haven't done you any good so far."

"Fair instincts, though. You figured it would come back someplace it already fed, and you were right. Only a couple miles off-target, and who knew the famous big-game hunter couldn't take care of himself."

"Before we go," Thorn said, "I'd like to have a word with Mr. Butterfield."

"Don't see why not, unless Doc's potion put him under. Go across and tell the sawbones that I sent you. Shouldn't give you any grief about it."

"Right." Thorn stood and left some money on the table for his breakfast, with another dollar tip, and followed Brisbin from the restaurant. They parted there, Gideon moving toward the doctor's office, while Brisbin hurried along to rouse the undertaker and his sidekick, setting up whatever they would need to fetch the latest corpse.

Doc Wyman greeted Thorn, saying, "Lute told me that you might stop in, if he could find you."

"It's all right with you, then?"

"Fine. I gave him some potassium bromide, a kind of sedative. He's better now—not raving any more, at least—but still awake."

"What did you make of him when Marshal Brisbin brought him in?"

"I'd bet a year's pay that he witnessed something shocking. As to *what* it was, exactly, how reliable he was in his description...well, I couldn't say for sure. On top of which he'd had a couple drinks since seeing whatever it was, and smelled of it."

"But do you think it's something he imagined?"

"Might be, if he was going through delirium tremens, but he denied being drunk when he saw it. For me, finding a corpse like he described would be the clincher. From what Ezra said, this Lockhart fellow likely couldn't do it to himself, and Ezra was supposed to get the mine's machinery geared up. It stands idle at night, so I'd rule out that kind of accident."

"Okay. Where have you got him?"

"Follow me."

Wyman led him to a backroom where his patient lay mostly in shadow, curtain filtering the morning light. The man was still awake, head turned to eye Thorn with suspicion.

"Mr. Butterfield?" Thorn asked.

"Nossir."

Thorn frowned. "No?"

"Mr. Butterfield would be my pappy. I'm just Ezra. Ever'body calls me that. You might as well."

"Well, thank you, Ezra. I'm Gideon Thorn, trying to help your marshal out with what's been happening lately."

"Same thing that Lockhart fella said. Now look at him."

"I plan to. But I thought we'd have a quick word first, if you don't mind."

"Go on ahead. But I already told the marshal what I seen."

"I'd like to hear it for myself, if that's all right."

"Okay. Why not?"

At first, it seemed that Butterfield was waiting for an invitation to proceed, but then he launched into it, saying, "Ain't a lot to tell, and likely nothin' that'll help ya. I went out like every other morning, to get things set up at the Elvira, but I never got around to it. Ya know, this be the *second* time I found a dead 'un at the mine. Startin' to think I need another job."

"You found the last watchman?"

"Tha's a fact. All by my lonesome—and I tell you, it *is* lonesome out there, first thing in the mornin'. They'll likely want me for the watchman next, but they can take that job and shove it where the moon don't shine."

"About this morning..."

"Right. So, I take my gun like ever' mornin' since I found poor Garth. 'Course, he was back a ways into the adit, but the thing that kilt Lockhart was too hungry to wait, I guess."

Thorn prodded him. "You were approaching when you saw...?"

"The damnedest thing I ever clapped eyes on, believe me. And I never hope to see its like again, in this world or the next 'un."

"If you could describe it..."

"Not too well. There weren't much moonlight, but just enough to see that it were big and dark. My guess is black or gray, somethin' like that, but you can't hold me to it."

"No. I won't."

"So, I come ridin' up and see this pile a somethin' liyin' next to one of the mine carts, but kind of *movin'* like, if you can pitcher it. Ripplin' around like canvas with somebody stuck beneath it, like. I guess it heard me comin', cuz it raised a head with red eyes blazin' from what light there was, comin' from Lockhart's little shack."

"Can you describe its face?"

"Them red eyes was the only thing I seen before it gave this screechin' noise, like rusty hinges openin'. Next thing I know, it's flappin' off and outa there on big, dark wings. I'd guess they musta been twelve, fifteen feet across, but Marshal Brisbin and the doc, here, reckon I was just in shock."

"Go on, please."

"Ain't much more to say. I woulda turned around and rid away first thing, but I seen someone lyin' on the ground there. It was Jeb, o' course, all mangled. He's the second watchman I found dead, and there ain't gonna be no third."

"Ezra could use some rest now," Dr. Wyman interjected, from the doorway. If you don't mind, Mr. Thorn..."

"Just one more question. Ezra, if you can remember, were the injuries you saw on Mr. Lockhart and the man before him—"

"Garth."

"Right. Did you find them more or less the same?"

"Mostly, from what I seen afore I hauled ass outa there —except for one thing, now you mention it."

"Which was?"

"Instead a just his neck torn open, looked like Mr. Lockhart lost part of his foot. Don't that beat all?"

Lute Brisbin had collected undertaker Mullins and Othaniel Morley by the time Thorn met them on the street, with Dr. Wyman following. Mullins was lean and middle-aged, a gray man from his hair to his complexion and his suit. Morley was young, as advertised, well built for his age, with old eyes in a round, red, pimply face beneath brown hair that hadn't met a morning comb. Thorn guessed he'd seen plenty of death already, working for Gus Mullins, with the recent killings piled on top of that.

Some way to spend your in-between years, handling corpses, but to each his own.

Mullins and Morley occupied the high seat of a horse-drawn wagon, with two mares—a dapple gray and a grulla—in harness, Morley on the reins. They had a plain pine casket lying in the wagon's bed, its lid off to one side. Marshal Brisbin was mounted on the dun gelding from yesterday and looming over Thorn.

"Learn anything from Ezra?" he asked, while Wyman clambered up onto the wagon seat.

"Not much. Red eyes, big wings. He's tired of finding corpses in the morning. Looking for another job, I'd say."

"Don't blame him. I was gonna get your stallion saddled up, but he was acting scrappy."

"Shadow doesn't take to strangers. You all go ahead and I'll catch up."

"Reckon you know the way," Brisbin replied, then told the wagon's passengers, "Let's get on to it."

Thorn jogged to the livery, paid off the hostler for another night, and got his animals calmed down. Belle, to be honest, wasn't too upset, but Shadow was a one-man horse and likely would've flattened Brisbin if the marshal had been fool enough to try dragging him from his stall.

Ten minutes later, Thorn was headed out of town and northward, letting Shadow run until he saw the wagon and its escort rider up ahead. He overtook them easily and Shadow fell in step beside the marshal's dun, shooting a sidelong glance at Brisbin as if telling him, "See how it's done?"

The first few mines they passed, aboveground workers slacked off to observe the grim procession, foremen barking at them to stop lollygagging and get busy. When they got to the Elvira, work was stalled, nothing the man in charge could say to prod his miners down the open shaft. Up on the crag above them, three vultures sat watching, obviously hoping those still capable of movement would clear out and leave their breakfast where it lay.

Win Cowan stood beside the twisted corpse of Jeb Lockhart, fanning at blowflies with his hat and looking sour.

"Christ, you could've covered him, at least," Brisbin complained, as he dismounted.

"Didn't think to bring no blanket out from home—not that Cherry woulda let me mess one up, regardless—and this bunch can't spare a tarpaulin." As he spoke, Win cocked a scornful thumb toward the assembled gawkers.

"We have something," Mullins said, turning around to face the casket, reaching down inside it.

"Hold on now," Brisbin instructed, "till we have a look at him."

Standing over the man he'd last seen living, exiting the

Lucky Strike saloon, Thorn viewed the mutilation at his throat, torn deep enough to set his head askew on what remained of Lockhart's neck. Aside from being dusty, seeming vaguely flat, like every other corpse Thorn could remember, there appeared to be no other injuries between the bounty hunter's throat and his right foot. Down there—

"He done that to hisself," said Cowan. "Had that fancy gun, there, but it didn't do no good. Both barrels fired, but didn't hit nothin' except his own damn foot."

"Looks like the ten-gauge did that," Brisbin said.

"No doubt," Doc Wyman answered. "And from what I see, his neck wound is the same as all the other ones I've seen so far. Just let me measure it, before you load him up."

Wyman removed a rolled-up tape measure from one of his pockets and crouched beside the corpse's left shoulder, checking the fatal bite's diameter, then working out circumference while trying not to stain his tape or fingers with what blood remained.

"Goddamn these flies," he muttered, rising to full height. "Well, if it helps you, Marshal, I make that five and a quarter inches wide, eight and a half around. Since it's the freshest wound I've seen, call that the average."

"And blood gone like the rest, I take it?" Brisbin asked.

Wyman nodded, saying, "Best I can tell, without a more in-depth examination."

"Right. Well, you can do that back at your place, Doc, and let me know. Ready for Gus to box him up?"

"As far as I'm concerned," the doctor answered.

"Hold up," Thorn said. "What's that, down by his right boot where it's blown away?"

"I didn't notice that," Wyman replied, taking a knee beside the corpse's feet and fanning off more flies.

The ten-gauge blast had shorn off roughly half of

Lockhart's boot and all his toes along with it, spilling more blood than had congealed around the dead man's violated throat. *Because his heart was pumping when he shot himself,* Gideon thought, *before whatever killed him got to draining him.*

What he had spotted on the leg of Lockhart's denim jeans appeared to be a stain at first, blown back from when his foot exploded, but a second look told Thorn that it was something else. Now, as he watched, Doc Wyman pulled a pair of tweezers from another pocket, peeling back and lifting up a dark brown scrap of some material and backing off, to study it without a swarm of flies intruding.

"Well, Doc," Brisbin nagged him. "What'n hell *is* that?"

"It's skin," the doctor said at last. "Or hide, if you prefer, apparently peeled off whatever took him down. Seems Mr. Lockhart grazed the creature he was hunting, after all."

"Fat lotta good it did him," Brisbin groused.

"It may do us some good, though," Wyman answered back. "You see this bristly hair?" He held the bloody sample up for better viewing, but the marshal flinched away from it.

"Went off without my specs," said Brisbin.

Wyman blinked at him and said, "I've never seen you wearing glasses, Lute."

"Never mind that. There any chance that you can tell us what that came from?"

"I can use the microscope, back at my office," Wyman said. "It's definitely skin, but whether I can match it to a given animal without a bigger sample, preferably a whole specimen, I just can't say."

"Whole specimen," the lawman muttered. "All we need to do is find and kill the damned thing, then."

"Bearing in mind it probably has friends," Wyman added.

"Thanks for reminding me."

Thorn watched Wyman extract an envelope from yet another pocket, drop the skin sample inside and put the tweezers with it, folding up the envelope before he stashed it out of sight.

"Ready for us, then?" Gus Mullins asked Marshal Brisbin.

"He's all yours."

Mullins and Morley climbed down from the wagon's seat and walked around behind it, lowering the tailgate. Morley pulled the casket closer, while his boss retrieved a folded wad of sailcloth, opening it with his young aide's help as they approached the corpse. When it was shaken out, they spread it on the ground, then rolled Jeb Lockhart onto it and swaddled him, hoisting his weight between them and retreating toward the wagon.

"Let us help you," Brisbin told them. Adding, "Win, come on."

"Jesus, I gotta lug him now?"

"Or you can ride on back to town and find yourself another job," his boss replied.

"Hey, it was just a question, Lute."

"And I gave you the answer."

Thorn saw that if he tried helping them, he'd only make things worse. Sometimes, eight hands are plenty; adding more just makes a mess of it. Doc Wyman seemed to share that view, moving to stand beside Thorn as the others situated Lockhart's gift-wrapped body in the coffin, set the lid on top without securing it, and closed the wagon's tailgate once again.

Morley scrambled back to the driver's seat, while

Mullins asked the lawman, "Do you know of any family he might've had, Marshal?"

"Can't say I do," Brisbin replied. "I'll wire Phil Rutter in Tucson and find out what he knows. He'll likely want to come down anyway and raise some hell about this holding up production."

"If he wants to hire another watchman," Thorn chimed in, "tell him that Ezra Butterfield says, 'No'."

"Don't blame him," Brisbin said. He mounted up, and Thorn did likewise, pleased that Shadow hadn't shied away from Lockhart's body or the watchers, though the swarm of blowflies plainly irritated him. The stallion huffed and flicked his tail in warning to the buzzing pests.

"You know Sheriff Shibell will try to put the blame for this on me."

"That's ludicrous," Thorn said.

"It's what he does, our Charley. Dump a job on someone else, then wash his hands of it when something goes amiss."

"And voters keep electing him?"

"What can I say? He's handsome, I suppose, and definitely has the gift of gab. He butters up the moneymen and does 'em favors any time he can. Chases an outlaw now and then, for show, leaving his deputies to do the dirty work."

"How do you really feel?" asked Thorn, half-teasing.

"Don't mind me. These killings have me in a funk, and I suspect I'm gonna lose my badge before they're solved."

"Afraid I haven't helped you much, so far," Thorn said.

"Don't let it worry you. You've only been in town a day."

"And wasted last night sitting out at Simon Cain's."

"You had it right, though, if you think about it."

"How's that?"

"The goddamned thing came back to an old haunt, all right. Just not the one you had staked out."

Thorn saw the truth in that. His guess had nearly paid off, but it wasn't good enough. To crack this riddle, he must first identify the animal, then start to think ahead of it.

It was a race, and so far, he was still stuck at the starting line.

SEVEN

Thorn was accustomed to most forms of violent death by personal experience, and while it never pleased him, either as an onlooker or a participant, it no longer had any negative impact upon his sleep or appetite. Leaving the livery, after assuring Shadow they'd be going out again that evening, Gideon realized that he was hungry and resolved to deal with that.

After his breakfast at the Mother Lode, he chose Delmonico's for lunch, trying to spread his custom evenly between the two establishments, and at the same time, keep his movements in Montana Camp from seeming too predictable. A new waitress placed him with a view of the street, table for two with one chair empty, and she handed him another shopworn menu that he hadn't seen before.

Thorn felt like Mexican today, ordering what they called the combination platter: one taco heaped high with chorizo, cheese, and lettuce; a tamale made with shredded pork and chili peppers; a chile relleno; refried beans; and *arroz con lima,* which proved to be lemon-flavored rice. He dug into the meal enthusiastically, drinking a large and frosty mug of beer to cool his tongue between spicy mouthfuls.

When he was done, he ambled to Doc Wyman's office, found some would-be patients in the waiting room, and waited for the doctor to emerge from somewhere at the rear.

"Ah, Mr. Thorn," said Wyman, greeting him.

"Just 'Gideon,' like Ezra," Thorn replied. "Speaking of which, how it he?"

"Gone home, once he slept a bit. No injuries that I could treat with medicine or bandages. If nightmares start to bother him, I guess he'll have to work that out himself."

"Uh-huh. And what about that skin from Lockhart's pants?"

"Wish I could tell you more than what I mentioned at the scene, but as it is, I'm stumped. Under the microscope, I verified it isn't human, but we knew that, going in. The hair is brown and wiry, sparse on whatever part of the creature's body it was flayed from. There's a trace of blood on it, also not human, but beyond that..."

"No clue as to species?"

"Don't I wish? If it was smaller, I'd suspect it's from some rodent, but from what I see, there's nothing like it living in the Territory. We've got pack rats, several kinds of mice. The so-called roof rats—what they call black rats back east, or ship rats if you find them on a boat at sea—grow up to eighteen inches long, but half of that is naked tail. To lose a swatch of hide like we found, one would likely have to die. And then, of course, there's no question of one doing the damage seen on Lockhart or the other victims, much less all the livestock. Any steer would likely trample one to death."

"I've heard about a larger rodent, four feet long or

better, standing up to two feet at the shoulder," Thorn replied.

"Ah. That would be the capybara. If you want to find one, ride through Mexico, on down to South America, and look around their rivers, lakes, or swamps and such. On top of which, they're strictly herbivores, living on grass, aquatic plants, tree bark and fruit."

"So, not man-eaters, then."

"Not even close. Sorry."

"By process of elimination, can you think of anything that's left?"

The doctor shook his head. Said, "I'm fresh out of notions on this one."

"All right."

"I understand you talked to Dr. Müller out at his place."

"With the marshal, right."

"He couldn't help with any insight?"

"*Nada,*" Thorn replied, his recent feast turning his mind toward Spanish for a second. "Says he does all his experiments on worms and tadpoles, watching them develop, fiddling around with them to see what make their evolution tick."

"Don't mention evolution to our preacher, if you happen to meet him. Reverend Belcher thinks Charles Darwin is the antichrist."

"Reverend *Belcher*?"

"Ellwood Belcher, Came to grace us from some holler in Missouri, with the emphasis on 'holler'."

Thorn had to laugh at that, was still appreciating it when Wyman asked, "So, what's your next step, hunting for these things?"

Gideon said, "I need to get a map of the vicinity, the largest scale available. Know where I might find one?"

"The marshal's got one at his office. Otherwise, you'd have to try the county courthouse up in Tucson."

"It's the marshal, then," Gideon said.

"What's on your mind?"

"I'm not sure yet, but I'll keep you advised."

Lute Brisbin was behind his desk when Thorn entered the office, glancing up from a report he'd been completing on the latest homicide.

"You get a lead on Lockhart's next-of-kin?" Thorn asked.

"Nothing so far. It's like he sprouted from a cabbage patch. Phil Rutter's on his way down here, like I predicted, with a couple of his men. His telegram announcing it says he knows nothing about Lockhart beyond how he claimed to be a first-rate hunter. Now, at least, he won't have to pay Lockhart's salary for doing nothing at the mine."

"I guess it's natural he'd want to check up on the crew that's still alive," Thorn said.

"I doubt he worries much about their well-being," Brisbin replied. "He's fired miners for getting hurt so bad they can't report for work. My guess would be, he wants to throw his weight around, remind me of how rich he is and all the bosom friends he has in Tucson, not to mention at the capital in Phoenix. He might fire the foreman who's been working for him eighteen months, and likely try to light a fire under my ass for what he calls incompetence or insubordination. If he starts on me, I swear—"

"You work for him?"

"No, Sir. But Sheriff Charley names the local lawmen, though we aren't exactly deputies of his. That way, he figures that we owe him for the job and have to take the heat whenever anything goes wrong. *He* has to get elected every four years, and that means keeping the money men on his side, come what may."

"Sounds like the system's rigged against you."

"Amen, brother, but that's my own cross to bear. What brings you by?"

"Doc Wyman says you have a good map of the territory hereabouts."

"He's right." Brisbin got up, crossed to a cupboard set beside his gun rack, and removed a rolled-up paper tube. Returning to his desk he spread the map and took a moment weighting down its corners with an inkwell, metal knuckles, and a pocketknife, so that it wouldn't curl back on itself.

"What are you looking for?"

"I'd start with the locations of the points where raids have taken place, and maybe mark them with a pencil."

"Can do," Brisbin said, and started pointing out locations all around Montana Camp, drawing a small X over each one. As he worked, the lawman named them. "Simon Cain's place sits right here...and this was Farnum's spread...and here is the Elvira mine. That's all the places where these goddamned things killed *people,* but they also slaughtered livestock here...and here...about right here...and over here."

When Lute was done marking the map, he'd sketched a rough circle around Montana Camp, ten or twelve miles across by Thorn's mental arithmetic, but with substantial gaps showing around its fifty-something-mile circumference.

"Damn. I was hoping for a smaller area to cover," Gideon remarked.

"Welcome to my hellhole," said Brisbin.

"Well, I'll have to work with what we've got."

"Meaning?"

"It stands to reason that if these killers are animals, they've got to have a nest somewhere nearby. And if they're capable of any thinking we'd call logical, they won't take victims right around their lair. Since we're supposing they can fly, based on what Ezra Butterfield reports he saw, they could be covering a fair amount of ground when they go hunting."

"And it's always after dark," Brisbin reminded him.

"Correct. They'd leave the nest around sundown, fly overland until they spot a source of food, then feed and double back."

"So, if I follow you, there'd be no raids too close around the nest."

"Unless they've killed off all the handy food across their wider range."

"I'm hoping it won't come to that."

"You and me, both."

"All right, what are we looking for?"

"A place where animals of a substantial size can hide during the daylight hours. An abandoned barn would be a long shot, since they'd likely catch the scent of men and worry someone might surprise them while they're sleeping."

"If they *do* sleep," Brisbin added.

"Any living thing I've ever heard of needs to sleep sometime. Nocturnal hunters lay up when the sun's out, daytime hunters overnight."

"We have a couple of abandoned ranches, barns still standing, but if they don't count—"

"Maybe a cave or something similar. Remember, Dr.

Wyman thinks we're dealing with at least four of these creatures, maybe more, based on his measurement of bite marks."

"I don't know of any caves nearby, although I haven't spent time prowling in the Atascosa Mountains, which are closest to Montana Camp."

"How much ground do they cover?"

"I make it thirty-odd square miles, the tallest of 'em being Atascosa Peak, above six thousand feet."

"We haven't got the manpower to sweep all that," Thorn said. "And looking at your map, the nest or whatever you want to call it should be somewhere closer to the town."

"So, definitely no caves that I ever heard of, then," Brisbin replied. "But we've got some abandoned mineshafts, where the claims played out and people working them moved on."

"That's better. Searchers should be able to examine them with lamps or torches during daylight."

"If they *will,*" Brisbin countered. "Folks here in town are right riled up, as you'd imagine. Going down into dark holes to hunt for monsters isn't high on anybody's list of things to do right now."

"If you and I do it alone, it will take...what, a week?"

"That oughta do it, but I don't like thinking of who gets killed in the meantime."

"No." Another thought occurred to Thorn. "Have there been any killings, stock or humans, on the reservation?"

"Now, see, that's another problem," Brisbin said. "First thing, the rez covers something like forty-five thousand square miles. On top of that, the Papagos—or Tohono O'odham Nation, as they call themselves—are governed by a tribal council ratified from Washington."

"Does that include for purposes of law enforcement?"

"For local matters, yes, things like killings within the tribe, sometimes a rape, or simpler things like thievery. If problems from the rez slop over to the white world, then you're dealing with the almighty Bureau of Indian Affairs, which has its own police force. And if *they* can't handle whatever comes up, we've got the U.S. Army at Fort Thomas, on the Gila River. That's two hundred miles northwest of where we're standing. There's supposed to be a closer camp at Fort Huachuca, opening sometime this month. That cuts down the ride to eighty-odd miles, but it isn't staffed with soldiers yet."

"And I'm guessing the commander at Fort Thomas—"

"Captain Clarence Mitchell."

"—doesn't like to send his troops that far from base."

"You'd win that bet."

"What do we do about the reservation, then?" Thorn asked.

"I've got no jurisdiction there," said Brisbin, "but I *can* ride out and ask some questions of the elders. That is, if they don't get all het up and run me off."

"It couldn't hurt," Thorn said.

"Unless they take more serious offense. But what the hell, I'll likely have no job this time next week."

"There's that." Thorn asked, "How long until this Rutter character shows up?"

"Depends on how hard he's pushing his horses. Call it eight, nine hours, anytime from half-past six to seven thirty would be my surmise."

"I'll hang around until he gets here, try to back you up if he comes on too strong."

"Strong is the only way he ever comes on," Brisbin said.

"When you say hang around till then, have you got more plans for tonight?"

"Another hunt. If I can bag one of the creatures, it'll be a leg up on our mystery. And if I can't, maybe we'll take a ride out to the reservation."

"Both of us?"

"Safety in numbers, eh?"

"If you call two a number. Never won a poker hand holding a single deuce, myself."

"Maybe you need to work on bluffing."

"Right. That must be it."

"Before I go, you mentioned sending telegrams from here. Where would I find the Western Union office?"

"Next-door to the Lucky Strike saloon."

"Got it."

"Something related to our problem here?"

"Might be," Thorn said. "But it's a long, *long* shot. Playing a hunch that likely won't pan out."

"Well, good luck to us both. You want to spot Phil Rutter when he gets here, keep your eye out for a fancy buckboard with a driver for His Majesty, likely a couple shooters covering him. You'll know him from his height, at five foot nothing, and his red face underneath a big straw hat. The red's mostly from booze and blood pressure, not working in the sun. If you can't tell him any other way, he'll be the one yelling at me."

"I'll be here," Thorn repeated, and went out into the street, walking along until he passed the Lucky Strike and found the Western Union office, barely large enough to rate being referred to as a shed. The company wasn't wasting its hard-earned money on Montana Camp.

Inside, he found a fifty-something clerk dressed in the standard uniform: a peaked cap on his head, a double-breasted jacket buttoned all the way up to its military collar, desert heat be damned. This clerk had sweated through his coat, under the sleeves, and from the look of it, today wasn't the first time, either.

"Help you, Sir?"

"I need to send a wire."

The narrow smile stopped short of mockery. "You've come to the right place, then. Going where, Sir?"

"Austria. Vienna, more specifically."

"Vienna's a large city, Sir. If you could tell me something more..."

"Address it to their university."

"All right."

He pushed a blank form and a three-inch pencil stub across the counter. Thorn considered what he had to ask and kept it on the cryptic side, not wishing to arouse any undue suspicion if it wasn't warranted but saying just enough to hopefully elicit an informative response. It was a fine line and it took some time, but when he finished, Gideon was satisfied with the result.

What were the odds against him getting any kind of answer? Speculating, he supposed they must be three or four to one. Why would a stranger who had never heard of him wire back at all" And if he did, what could he say to help resolve a lethal mystery across nearly ten thousand miles of land and sea?

When he was finished, Thorn returned the filled-out form and pencil to the Western Union clerk. The older man read over it, nodding as if he understood the importance of it, Gideon reckoned it was clear as mud to him.

"Addressed to a Professor...should that name be 'Gregory'?"

"No," Gideon replied. There was no point in flaunting

any of his Harvard education to this fellow in a dead-end job. "I looked it up. It's spelled the way you see it there."

"Just as you say, Sir. And the price tag for a transatlantic message of this length will be..."

The figure that he quoted would've seemed prohibitive to most farmers and shopkeepers around Montana Camp. The clerk's gray eyebrows arched when Thorn dipped in a pocket of his vest and counted out the sum in cash.

"And I'll be needing a receipt for that," Gideon said.

"Of course, Sir. Right away."

"How long between transmission and delivery, if you can estimate?"

The clerk referred to a wall-mounted chart of global time zones. "Austria is nine hours ahead of us," he said. "I'll send this straightaway, which routes it out of Tucson to New York City. Vienna should receive it close to two o'clock tomorrow morning, but they won't be waking anybody up at that hour, particularly members of a college faculty. My best guess—and it's *just* a guess, mind you—would be sometime mid-morning over there, say nine or ten o'clock on Monday. Call it midnight here, or maybe one o'clock."

"And any answer coming back?" Thorn had already done the math, but wanted confirmation, just in case his party opted to respond.

"Dial back nine hours from delivery, unless your wire finds the recipient tied up with classes or what-have-you. We don't open for business here until seven o'clock, of course, so make it thirteen, maybe fourteen hours from now, at the soonest."

"Anytime from seven until noon, then."

"*If* the person who you're contacting responds. We can't control that end of things, you understand. There is no obligation to reply, of course."

"Of course. And if he does, you'll send any response on to the Copper Queen, in care of me?"

"Yes, sir. Weekdays, we have a boy who handles that, assuming I can find him."

Thorn imagined that the kid in question might be stuck in school himself, or finding other ways to earn a pittance in between rare telegrams.

"Just do your best."

"Yes, Sir. We always aim to please."

Thorn left and started walking back to his hotel. Another nap to tide him through the night ahead, then supper at Delmonico's, before he circled back to Marshal Brisbin's office for a look at this Phil Rutter character. Gideon didn't like the sound of him, but tried to keep an open mind, remembering he'd only heard Brisbin's description of the mine owner.

If he was anything like George Hearst, whom Thorn had collided with in Texas some time back, there was a chance of sparks flying between them, but he had to think of Brisbin first and foremost, striving not to undercut the marshal's status by promoting an unnecessary feud. If need be, he could always try to work around Rutter, ignore whatever ultimatums he handed to Brisbin, operating from the knowledge that he had no hold on Gideon, no power over him.

As for his long-shot telegram, Thorn wasn't counting on a helpful answer—hell, or *any* answer, if it came to that. He knew the man on the receiving end had never heard of him and likely wouldn't care what happened in a tiny Arizona town, assuming that he managed to believe Thorn's short and rather cryptic explanation. Still, it had been worth a try.

Unbidden, Gideon's thoughts turned to Dinah Pilcher,

wondering where she was now, what she was doing, and with whom she might be doing it. He missed her company more than he wanted to admit, and wished her well in any new endeavor she attempted. As for writing any more about his life and its macabre cases, he wouldn't mind if she abandoned that and let him travel on in peace.

But missing her? Yes, definitely. Thorn couldn't deny that, even to himself.

EIGHT

Delmonico's had more diners than Gideon was used to seeing on his prior visits, several of them eyeing him with no attempt to hide it. Thorn couldn't decide if gossips had begun to spread his about reputation, maybe some exaggerated version of it, through Montana Camp, or else they were expecting Phil Rutter to show up in their midst. Maybe they'd mistaken him for one of Rutter's bodyguards.

In any case, he gave them back cold eyes, discouraging any attempts at conversation, while the waitress showed him to a table on the south side of the dining room and left him with a menu that had roast beef added to the offerings from lunch. Thorn went for that, with fried potatoes on the side and biscuits once again, sipping his coffee while he waited for his meal to be prepared.

He knew nothing of Rutter beyond what the marshal had related to him earlier, none of it flattering. The best course, Thorn decided, was to drop by Brisbin's office as if uninvited, see the man up close and make his own judgment before he closed the book and stuck it back up on its shelf.

Worst case scenario: the mine owner would prove to be a loud, insufferable ass, the kind of businessman with whom Thorn was familiar from his personal experience in Boston and points west. If that proved true, it might mean complications for his hunt, especially if Lute Brisbin tucked tail and called Thorn off the case.

Of course, he didn't really work for Brisbin, either, so he couldn't just be fired when he was acting privately, not under contract or receiving any salary. If Brisbin wanted to get rid of him, he'd have to fabricate some charge and either run Thorn out of town—pointless, since he could camp outside the marshal's jurisdiction and proceed alone—or try to lock him up, another losing proposition that would only make the lawman seem more ineffectual and weak to his constituents.

Thorn checked his pocket watch before he settled up his bill and left a tip. The hour was 6:25, and Rutter's party should be turning up at any time within the hour to confront Montana Camp's lawman.

As if in answer to his thoughts, Thorn left Delmonico's to find a stylish buckboard with a driver and a single passenger proceeding south on the main street, slowing down as it approached the marshal's office. He knew Rutter from Brisbin's description of a red-faced, smallish man, dressed better than most men would bother for a trip across the Arizona desert.

At the buckboard's reins, a second man larger than Rutter, both in height and girth, was also dressed up in a suit, though cheaper than the boss's duds, his boots showing more wear than Rutter's polished brogues. Behind the buckboard, one to either side of it, rode two rough-looking customers on horseback. Neither one of them had bothered with a suit or tie, but each of them wore pistols on their hips and carried lever-action rifles in their saddle boots.

Thorn watched them pass and saw the driver pull up outside Brisbin's office, hopping down to give his boss a hand descending to the wooden sidewalk. Rutter's hard-eyed flankers both dismounted, tied their horses to a hitching rail nearby, and waited for their paymaster to disappear inside the office before staking out a handy bench to rest their legs.

Thorn crossed the street, passing behind the buckboard as he reached the sidewalk, homing in on Brisbin's door. One of the seated shooters called out to him, "Better try it later, friend. The marshal's got important company."

Thorn faced them down, then smiled and said, "I'm glad he waited for me."

He had one hand on the doorknob when the pair of them stood up and moved a little closer to him. The one who had spoken first now asked, "There something wrong with your ears, friend?"

Thorn stopped and brushed his frock coat back, revealing his twin Colts with hammer thongs unfastened. "First mistake," he said. "I'm not your friend and likely never will be. Second error is imagining that you can shade a stranger when you've never seen him work."

"In case your ears are worse than your eyesight," the mouthpiece said, "there's three of us and only one of you."

"Poor odds for you, I'd say," Thorn answered back. Without turning his head a bit, he told the buckboard's driver, "If you want to cut a slice of this, feel free. But first, all three of you should name your beneficiaries."

"Big talk," the braggart tried to sneer, but couldn't pull it off convincingly.

"So, make your move, *friend,*" Thorn replied.

Nobody moved for half a minute, so he turned the heat down, smiling at them, reaching for the door again. "Maybe another time," Thorn said. "I'll tell your boss I'm late because of you all. Do you think he'll appreciated it?"

They were chewing over that one as Thorn passed inside and shut the marshal's door behind him. Rutter had been saying something, bringing extra color into Brisbin's cheeks, but stopped and turned to glare at Gideon.

"We're busy here," he said. "You'd better run along."

"I'm where I need to be," Thorn said. "And it was rude of you, starting without me while your monkeys held me up."

Rutter narrowed the little rat's eyes in his crimson face. "And who in hell are you, that I'd even consider waiting for you. Mister..."

"Thorn. Gideon Thorn. I'm working with the marshal here to solve your little problem for you."

"You call a risk of shutting down my mine a *little problem*? I'd be forced to disagree—and who hired you for this job, anyway? On what authority."

"To take your questions in the order given," Thorn replied, "losing a couple of night watchmen while your mine keeps working all day long is tragedy to those dead men, but nothing much at all to you. Second, nobody *hired* me and nobody's paying me. I mostly work jobs of this kind for free."

"Oh, so you've handled other cases like this one?"

"More than you'd care to know about," Thorn said. "And third, I'm here by the authority of Marshal Brisbin. He's the only law in town, and since you live in Tucson, maybe you'd consider going home, getting the hell out of our way."

He thought Rutter might throw some kind of seizure

over that, but he controlled his temper with an effort, turning back to Brisbin. "I'm *not* used to being spoken to with such rank insubordination!"

Thorn answered before the marshal could. "No one inside this room is your subordinate," he said. "You'll find them on the sidewalk, waiting for you."

Spitting mad, Rutter told Lute, "Try grasping this, *Marshal.* My next stop is the sheriff's office for a word with Mr. Charles Shibell. You've heard of him, I take it?"

"Heard of 'im and had words with 'im on this very subject. My impression was he didn't give a damn. Thinks it's a bear, apparently. You see 'im, ask what kinda bear he knows of that can fly."

That startled Rutter into silence for a second, then he came back with, "You'll understand if I don't take your word for anything just now. But if I can't arouse the sheriff, it so happens that I'm good friends with Governor Safford."

"Old Anson. Can't say that news takes me by surprise. His friends still call him P. K.?" Half turning to Thorn, Lute said, "He's got two middle names, see: Pacely Killen."

"You make light of me at your peril, Mr. Brisbin. At the peril of your badge."

"You want it," Lute replied, "have Sheriff Charley or old P. K. pin it on your fancy vest. Until then, people who put trust in me are getting killed *right now,* and neither of your pals upstairs seems very much concerned. I'm doing what I can with what I've got, and you're wasting my precious time."

Rutter stormed out, flinging the door wide as he left and leaving it that way. One of his shooters tarried on the threshold, eyeing Gideon and pointing to him with an empty hand shaped like a pistol.

"Anytime you care to try it," Thorn advised him. "Now, you'd better run along."

The marshal took a moment to calm down, then forced a smile and said, "Well, that was fun, eh?"

"Do you think he'll go straight back to Tucson?" Gideon inquired.

"He's mad enough, but then again, it's getting on toward dark. Seventy miles across the desert with a waning moon, that wouldn't be the smartest thing he ever did."

Nodding, Thorn said, "I'd better get my hunting gear."

"You're going out again tonight?"

"Unless you have a better plan."

"If I had any goddamned plan at all, this mess would be behind us now," Lute said, broad shoulders slumping. "You be careful, now."

"I always am," Thorn said.

The four-man party clopped and clattered north along Bear Valley from Montana Camp. Full dark had overtaken them before the driver of Phil Rutter's buckboard asked him, "Are you *sure* you wouldn't rather double back, Sir? I imagine we could still get rooms at that hotel."

"Stop asking that, dammit!" his boss spat back. "If you can't handle this rig in the dark, give me the reins."

"No, Sir. I've got it. But it'll be well after midnight when we make it back to Tucson."

"I can tell time, Soames. My watch cost more than you make in a month."

One of the outriders snickered at that, and Rutter turned on him. "Something you want to say, Jackson? Or you, Friedman?" He spoke the latter's name as if it left a bad taste in his mouth.

They both replied in ragged unison, "No, Sir."

"We could stop off at the Elvira," Soames suggested.

"Right. And have my workers find me sleeping in a damned mineshaft when they turn out at dawn? That's brilliant. How about we all just lie down in the middle of the road?"

"No, Sir," his driver answered, adding, "It was just a thought."

"I do the thinking," Rutter said.

His cheeks still burned, and stomach acid still bedeviled him, riled up at how the so-called lawman and his lackey both had treated him with utter disrespect. Rutter knew that he should've stopped at one of the town's restaurants to eat a bite and let himself calm down, but all he'd wanted was to get the hell out of Montana Camp—and who could even trust their lousy food? The way his luck was going, Rutter thought he likely would've caught ptomaine. Even if he only got the runs, that would be bad enough to literally cap his rotten day with shit.

None of his hirelings spoke again as they rode on past the Elvira and a couple of the played-out mines he planned on picking up with paltry offers in another couple months. He was a mining man at heart, and knew that just because a mine appeared to be worn out, that didn't mean a smart man, paying diggers on the cheap, couldn't extract a tidy profit from somebody else's failure. He'd just let the shafts sit idle for a bit more time, and then—

An eerie, drawn out screech stabbed Rutter's eardrums, reaching him from somewhere overhead. He stiffened, craned his neck, scanning the darkness that surrounded them.

"The hell was that?" Jackson asked no one in particular.

"Some kinda night bird," Soames replied. "The desert's full of them."

"I never heard nothin' like that afore," Friedman chimed in.

"You spend your nights indoors and in your cups," Soames said, "missing all kinds of things."

"You jealous, Billy Boy?" Friedman retorted, but there was a tremor in his sneer.

Phil Rutter had begun regretting his impetuous decision to storm out of town in such high dudgeon. Now, he wished they *had* slept over at the Copper Queen hotel, getting a fresh start in the morning, traveling by full daylight.

Too late for that, he thought, and tucked a hand into the pocket of his coat, where he kept a Colt New Line revolver, its five-shot cylinder loaded with .38-caliber rounds. Just touching it normally increased his confidence, but now, surrounded by the night that stretched forever...

Screeeech! The sound was louder, closer that time.

"What 'n hell *is* that?" Jackson fairly whined.

"I told you once—"

"Close your pie hole, Soames! Screw you and your night bird."

"Shut up, the lot of you!" barked Rutter. "We should find out what that is."

"Sir—"

"Quiet, Soames! If that's a bird, it has to be the biggest one on Earth, and it sounds *close*."

As if to make a liar of him, yet another high-pitched squeal rang out, this one farther away but drawing nearer by the sound of it. Before the frightened men could speak again, a third note sounded from somewhere behind them, back toward the Elvira but approaching.

"Shit! They're all around us!" Jackson blurted out.

"Just show me one and I can drop it," Friedman growled, cocking his lever-action Winchester.

"No shooting yet, dammit!" Rutter ordered. "You'd likely pick off one another in the dark."

"I hit what I aim at," Jackson replied, sounding offended by the boss doubting his marksmanship.

"I said *no shooting,*" Rutter raged, then found he'd drawn his pocket Colt and cocked it without noticing.

Phil Rutter hated being frightened. As a child, he'd known the feeling well, facing his father's weekly drunken rages and the taunts of schoolyard bullies he could never quite stand up to. Time and shady business acumen had cured most of that, but there were still days when he felt the old, familiar fear, as if knowing he wasn't truly good enough to deal with larger, stronger men. Thankfully, he had learned to bludgeon them with money, with the weight of influential friends, and with the gunmen he kept at his beck and call.

Tonight, though, Rutter had a sickly feeling that all bets were off.

There was no screech the next time, but a flapping sound like sheets hung on a clothesline, caught by a stiff breeze. The sound came from Phil Rutter's left, passed so close overhead he ducked and missed his chance to see it go, but Heck Jackson was quicker, cranking off a shot from his Winchester that reverberated through the desert night.

Rutter spun toward him, shouting, "Jesus Christ! What part of 'no shooting' are you too fucking dumb to understand?"

But damned if Jackson wasn't grinning in the faint starlight. "I think I hit it, Boss. Winged it, at least. I—"

Whatever Heck meant to say was lost forever, when a pitch-dark portion of the night rushed toward him from behind, enveloped him, and snatched him from his saddle. Jackson just had time to wail, a pained and hopeless sound, before he vanished into darkness, somewhere overhead.

Sol Friedman was the next to fire, a random rifle shot at nothing visible, before he sputtered, "Hell with this!" and wheeled his mount around, spurring it to a gallop, back toward town. Rutter lost sight of him almost immediately, but he heard his erstwhile bodyguard screaming as something fell upon him from the night sky.

Friedman's horse was screaming too, in its own way. Rutter imagined man and animal dying together in a hot rush, slain by who-knew-what, and had to swallow back a rising laugh that felt too much like plain hysteria.

"Soames!"

"Yes, Sir!"

The driver had been quicker on the uptake, thinking clearer than his boss, lashing the reins at matched horses who were already anxious to clear out of there. Wild-eyed, hooves hammering, they galloped north along Bear Canyon, while the buckboard rocked and jolted after them. With his free hand, Rutter clung to the seat beneath him, knowing he was finished if he tumbled out onto the hard-packed sand.

"Shotgun!" Soames said to him, like a mental defective spouting words that made no sense. "It's underneath the seat!"

Of course it was, Rutter recalled. *I bought the goddamned thing and put it there myself, for an emergency.*

And if this didn't qualify, what would?

Rutter returned the Colt to his pocket, time wasted there, and nearly pitched head foremost from his wobbling perch as he bent forward, groping blindly underneath the driver's seat to grasp the sawed-off scattergun concealed there. After a breathless eternity, he found it, raised the stubby gun, and thumbed both hammers back.

"Come on!" he muttered. "Come on back, you bastard. Get a taste of this!"

"Don't *call* it, Boss!" his driver fairly pleaded with him. "Don't do *that*!"

"You think the goddamned thing speaks English, Billy? Did it go to school, or—"

Something heavy landed in the backseat of the buckboard, bringing Rutter's head and gun around to meet it. Panic and the darkness blinded him to whatever it was, except that it was big and furious and snarling. Rutter raised the shotgun, knew he didn't really have to aim it at that range, but he was set on killing with his first shot, knowing that he wasn't only faced with one attacker.

Just as Rutter's finger curled around the shotgun's double triggers, something like a blacked-out ship's sail swept across in front of him, slapping the scattergun off to his right as he craned backwards in his seat. The weapon fired both barrels with a blast that stunned him, spattering his face and clothes with warm, thick mist.

Before he realized that he was dripping human blood and brains, Rutter blinked at the spot where Billy Soames was sitting a split-second earlier. His place was empty now, of course. The double shotgun blast had swept him from the driver's seat and clean out of the buckboard, nothing but an ugly smear remaining on the seat's upholstery.

At that moment, Rutter discovered that even the faintest moonlight turns fresh blood as black as pitch.

"Fuck me!" he blurted out, dropping the empty scatter-gun, knowing that he had to move *right now,* or else die where he sat.

Without another thought—at least, not a coherent one—Phil Rutter leapt out of the speeding buckboard, saw and felt it rushing on without him as he hit hard ground, the wind knocked out of him on impact, gasping desperately to recover from his fall in time.

In time for what?

Maybe to die, but not without a fight, by God.

Remembering the Colt still in his pocket, Rutter fumbled for it, tried to yank it free, and only then remembered that he'd left it cocked. The .38 went off before he'd cleared it, Rutter suddenly less frightened than disgusted with himself for being such an idiot.

He felt the hot slug burn across his sagging belly—too damned fat, and no time left for slimming down—then managed to roll over on his back, pistol in hand. The night seemed to be *swarming* overhead, but he supposed that must an illusion, after plunging from the buckboard, getting turned around and all.

No, there was something—more than one of them in fact—wheeling above him, soaring, circling, dropping lower in the dark and chattering among themselves.

So this is how it ends, Phil Rutter thought, and wished he understood the goddamned reason why.

Before the first great shadow settled down on top of him, he cocked the Colt again and put it in his mouth.

NINE

Gideon Thorn was coming up on the Elvira mine when darkness fell over Bear Valley. He'd left town after Phil Rutter's crew, guessing the boss was too wound up to spend the night in town, preferring to reach Tucson and begin his ritual of raising hell for Lute Brisbin.

And me? he wondered, then immediately shrugged it off.

He didn't fear the county sheriff, or the governor, if it came down to that. Together, they might find some way to ban him from the territory, but Thorn knew a U.S. Senator from Massachusetts and four of the Bay State's congressmen, who'd been supported in their various campaigns by money from his Aunt's estate. One of the representatives had also asked Thorn's help at ridding his transplanted daughter's home of ghosts in Kansas City, and had pledged undying gratitude as a result.

Just now, the main thing Gideon wished for was brighter moonlight to illuminate his path, but no amount of influence in Phoenix or in Washington could handle that. He took his time, letting his stallion watch for ruts and gopher holes, until the first shot brought them both up short.

It was the flat *crack* of a rifle, and another, followed swiftly by the *boom* of a shotgun, then two sharp pistol shots, the latter separated by a minute, give or take. Mixed in with the gunfire, he heard human screams, male voices strained to breaking from their owners' pain and fear.

By that time, Shadow had begun to gallop toward the sounds of battle. Under normal circumstances, Thorn would have suspected an ambush by highwaymen, but when were circumstances ever "normal" in his life? It *was* an ambush, he decided, but by nothing human, some nocturnal predator in quest of sustenance.

When he had roughly halved the distance, by dead reckoning, a horse ran past him in the opposite direction, pounding back along the dirt road toward Montana Camp. Gideon thought he recognized it, one of those Phil Rutter's useless triggermen had tied outside the marshal's office, but between its speed and the absence of light, he couldn't swear to it.

One thing was clear: the animal had lost its rider and it wasn't lingering to help the man.

To clear the way ahead of him a bit, Gideon drew his right-hand Colt and fired it once into the air. Shadow ignored it, anything but gun shy, as he charged ahead. Five minutes more, and Thorn saw Rutter's buckboard up ahead of him, no one inside it that his heightened senses could detect. There *were* two bodies sprawled beside the carriage, neither showing any signs of life, and Gideon reined Shadow in as he approached them.

To the buggy's left, he found a corpse nearly bisected by a close-range blast of buckshot, mangled innards coiling from the massive wound. Thorn recognized the driver's clothes on sight, the face averted from him by a brutal twist that turned the dead man's head halfway around, his throat town open by the now-familiar fangs.

Circling around the buckboard's tailgate, Thorn found Rutter stretched out on his back. Aside from damage to his throat, the short man's hat and upper cranium were blown away. A small revolver dangled from a corner of Phil Rutter's gaping mouth, as if it were a pipe he had been smoking when death called for him.

The buckboard's matched horses had died in harness with their throats ripped out, but from the blood pooling around them, Thorn guessed his arrival had prevented their butchers from feasting at leisure—or maybe, he supposed, they'd simply had their fill of blood before the final kills. As to the bodyguards and second horse that one of them had ridden into town that afternoon, there was no trace that Gideon's sharp eyes could pick out in the night.

Somewhere above him, already receding into distance, Thorn heard one long screech. He scanned the night sky, thought he caught a glimpse of something dark and nimble, blotting out stars as it flew away, but that could've been an illusion, and the maybe-shadow was too swift, too far away, for any accurate gunfire.

Another glance around the slaughter site showed Thorn his only course of action now. He could've loaded Rutter and his driver back into the buggy, likely bloodying himself from head to toe, but to what end? With two dead horses, the conveyance wasn't going anywhere. Likewise, he could waste hours searching for the absent gunmen, but to what end? Even if he found them, Shadow couldn't carry back two leaking corpses to Montana Camp.

No, he was left with only one clear course of action. He'd return to town and rouse the marshal, Dr. Wyman, then the undertaker and his sidekick, in that order. They would need time to prepare—collecting Wyman's gear, Gus Grissom's wagon and more caskets if he had them standing by, perhaps calling for reinforcements—and then return to view whatever still remained.

In Gideon's absence, he guessed coyotes might come sniffing at the carrion and try to feed. For all he knew, the airborne killers might return as well, to store up more blood for the night and day ahead of them. He couldn't deal with either of those possibilities just now, alone, unless he stood watch with the dead till dawn.

Dismissing that notion, he started back toward town, keeping his stallion to a gentle trot. The dead required no haste on his part, and he wouldn't risk his horse on their behalf when they had passed beyond all earthly help. Thorn doubted that some drifter would appear and try to loot the bodies of their guns or pocket cash—but if one did, good luck to him, with unseen killers on the wing.

Thorn reached Montana Camp some thirty minutes later, creeping up on nine o'clock. There was a lamp burning inside the marshal's office, and he found Win Cowan at his boss's desk, perusing WANTED posters slated for addition to the notice board. Cowan flinched as Gideon entered, but he tried to cover it and listened to the grim news from Bear Valley.

"I can go fetch Lute," he said when Thorn was done, "or tell you where he lives while I stay here."

"You'd better stay," Gideon said. "Something might happen while you're gone, and I have no authority to deal with it."

Nodding agreement, Cowan gave directions to the marshal's place, a small house set a block west of the town's main street, it's number—27—painted on a post out front. It took some banging on the door before Lute Brisbin answered, still in a shirt and trousers, looking like he'd gone to bed that way.

"Just fell asleep," Lute said, as he admitted Thorn to his untidy living room. "What's happened now?"

Thorn told him, watching Brisbin wince at his description of the massacre. When he was done, the marshal said, "Well, one good thing about it, anyway. Phil won't be whipping up the sheriff or the governor against me now."

"It still might have the same effect," Thorn answered him. "A loud-mouthed money man goes down, people he's been supporting want to know the reason why."

"That should be something," Brisbin said. "Wonder if Sheriff Charley will keep laying blame off on a bear?"

"We need to get the doctor and the undertaker," Gideon pressed on. "Two men are dead beyond question, but there's an outside chance the other two could be alive."

"I'd call that *way* outside. Suppose we'll have to try and find them," Brisbin said. "But if we can't, without their names, I can't even alert their next of kin."

"Someone at Rutter's office must know who they were, since they were on his payroll."

"Right. One problem solved, at least."

"The horse that passed me on my way north may have come back into town," said Thorn, "or passed straight through and kept on running. Somebody will likely find it when it gets tired out."

"Or those damned *things* will," Brisbin said, as if it were a curse.

"About the dead ones and the buckboard..."

"I'll take care of that. Jake from the livery can bring the buggy in and clear those carcasses out of the road, at least. Buzzards will have a treat, if the coyotes don't get to them first. I guess someone from Rutter's office will collect the buggy, by and by."

"All right, then. Do you want to rouse the doctor or the undertaker?"

"You take Wyman. Grissom's known to be a heavy sleeper, and with all these people getting killed, he'll likely be on edge, maybe packing a shooting iron."

"I'll leave you to it, then."

Gideon knew where Dr. Wyman lived, and pounded on his door until the sawbones answered, pulling up suspenders where he'd hurried into trousers, covering the union suit he slept in. Wyman heard Thorn out, shaking his head through all of it.

"Good Lord," he said at last. "Another four?"

"Most likely," Gideon confirmed. "Two dead, for sure. I couldn't stick around and scout all of creation for the other two."

"Let me get dressed." Still talking as he moved back toward his sleeping quarters, Wyman said, "We may need daylight to locate the missing, if we ever do. With predators that fly, I guess there's some slight chance they'd carry off their prey. Eagles and hawks all have a limit to the weight they're capable of lifting, but with these things... I mean, since we don't know what they are, it's unpredictable."

A thought occurred to Gideon. "It might be helpful, though."

"How's that?" asked Wyman, pulling on his coat and picking up his doctor's bag.

"Most forms of transportation leave their marks,"

Thorn said, "whether its footprints, drag marks, wagon tracks, whatever."

"You expect to find a trail across the sky?"

"Not in the sky, but maybe on the ground. If one of these things killed a man, then lifted him and flew away, I'd hope to find a trail of bloodstains, if we're lucky."

"Ah. Well, I suppose it's possible, but that depends on whether he was dead or living when the damned thing hoisted him. You know, the heart stops pumping and the blood flow is reduced dramatically. And if the thing *fed* on him first...well, then, there might be no blood left to speak of."

"Understood," Thorn said. "But just a few drops falling as it flew away could give us a direction, point us toward its lair."

"I'll keep my fingers crossed," Wyman replied, and they cleared out of there, pausing just long enough for him to lock the door.

Lute Brisbin must have managed to avoid a dozy showdown with Gus Grissom. Thorn and Dr. Wyman found the undertaker and his helper loading up their wagon in an alleyway behind the mortuary, four new caskets lying on their sides, jammed in together, filling up the wagon's bed.

"You must be going through a lot of these," Thorn said to Grissom.

"It's a living," Grissom answered back.

"For us, at least," Othaniel Morley cracked. "Gus has a carpenter in town who keeps us stocked in coffins, but he'll likely need more lumber soon."

Thorn didn't care for Morley's grin, but saw no point in

arguing about lack of respect for the departed. With the wagon's tailgate shut and latched, Wyman seated beside the undertaker as he'd been on their last journey to a death scene, they rode north and out of town.

"Much more of this," Brisbin told Thorn, "I might as well resign before Shibell can get around to firing me. Don't know what other town will want a lawman with my résumé, but I'm not fit for much of anything besides policing, if you wanna call it that."

"I wouldn't give up hope just yet," Thorn said.

"I guess *you* wouldn't, free to ride out anytime you like and put Montana Camp behind you, but I swore an oath."

"And you're upholding it. No one with any common sense could doubt it."

"So, I do my so-called best, but people keep on dying, others getting wiped out when their livestock's slaughtered. Offer my excuses to the dead and destitute, should I? Hell, I don't buy that line, myself."

"You're up against something that none of us has seen before, maybe something beyond human experience. Unless you caused the killings to begin with, none of it's your fault."

"But I get paid a salary to *stop* this kind of shit. Granted, it isn't much, but if I can't track down a killer big enough to carry off a man—much less a whole damned pack of them—what good am I?"

"Before you write your resignation, let's check out the latest evidence, shall we? After the sun comes up, we may find something in the nature of a lead."

"Or two more bodies, anyhow."

They rode in silence then, until they reached the ambush site. Thorn counted three coyotes scuttling off with chunks of flesh still clenched between their teeth and tried to touch their minds with his, willing them to stay out of rifle range. The answers he received were muddled: fear of man mixed up with hunger, and behind all that, a sense of dread that had the scavengers confused as badly as the men who had disturbed their feast.

"Ye gods and little fishes!" Brisbin muttered, while dismounting from his mouse dun gelding. "These poor bastards never had a chance."

"Look closer, and you'll see that both of them were shot," Thorn said.

Standing above Phil Rutter, Brisbin said, "This one looks like a suicide. Phil took his shot, instead of waiting for those things to snack on him."

"I've thought about the driver," Gideon replied. "I'm guessing Rutter killed him by mistake, grabbing a shotgun from beneath the seat up there. It would explain the way he fell, before the other things got hold of him."

"Makes sense to me," Lute said, peering into the buckboard's footwell. "And we've got the twelve-gauge here, right where Phil dropped it after it went off. No way of telling if it might've helped him, otherwise."

"An eight-gauge didn't save the day for Simon Cain," said Thorn.

"And Phil's two gun slicks are...just gone?"

"I couldn't spot them from the road," Thorn said. "We'll likely have to save the search till after sunrise."

Brisbin struck a match against the buckboard's side and used its light to check his pocket watch. "Another seven hours, more or less. God*damn* it all!"

"Meanwhile," Doc Wyman interjected, "we should get these others back to town"

"Right. Sure." The lawman moved to help the others hoist Phil Rutter off the ground and carry him to Grissom's wagon, where the undertaker got him swaddled in a blanket, then arranged the caskets so that two were lying flat, uncovered, while the other two were still on edge and flanking them. It struck Thorn as a good thing that they hadn't found four dead, since loading them aboard the wagon might have proved too much.

The driver's body was another problem, nearly severed at the beltline, sloppy vitals dangling, dropping loose, before he was folded into a blanket of his own. Harder to lift, as well, because he sagged and tried to come apart while he was being placed inside the box. When it was done, the casket lids loosely secured, the living took a breather and then started back toward town.

Most of Montana Camp had slept through all the ruckus, only one drunk from the Dry Gulch leaning on an upright beam outside the barroom, watching them pass by.

"Go home, Dean," Brisbin warned him with a glare.

"Marshal," the sot retorted, cackling, "I *am* home."

"Then get off the goddamn street and mind your business!"

"Hey, there's no need to—"

Thorn didn't hear the rest of it as they left Dean behind, lamenting Brisbin's treatment of him. Back at Grissom's mortuary, Thorn and Lute dismounted, while the others climbed down from the undertaker's wagon and began removing the two coffins with their mutilated occupants. Once the two boxes were inside, borne by their drafted pallbearers, Lute turned to Thorn and said, "I'd better get a wire off to the sheriff. If I let him know what's happened, maybe I can beat him to the punch."

"He can't blame you for this," Gideon said.

"Don't be so sure. What *should* be and what Sheriff Charley does can be two very different things."

TEN

Gideon's first time in the undertaker's parlor, he discovered a workroom in back with two tables that stood waist-high and separated by enough space for a man to move between them. Each was made of polished wood, heavily varnished to repel liquids, surrounded by tin gutters on three sides, with downspouts leading to round drains set in the concrete floor. There was a sink as well, and Thorn spotted a rolling tray with surgical instruments lined up across it. The whole place smelled of alcohol and what Thorn knew must be formaldehyde, a prime ingredient of the embalming fluids used in Europe and America the past few years.

And now, the smells of blood and other body fluids mingled with that atmosphere.

Lifting a dead man onto each of the two tables took some doing. Rutter's body was the easier to shift, though far from tidy. With his driver, whom nobody present seemed to know by name, it required concerted effort to pick up the corpse's nearly severed halves and lay them more or less in place. Removal of the victims' clothes was complicated by the start of rigor mortis setting in from the head downward, stiffening each muscle as it spread down toward the feet, but Mullins and his young apprentice went to work with scissors, cutting along seams and yanking severed fabric free in pieces.

Dr. Wyman had remained to check the bodies over, and despite all he had seen while serving in a frontier practice, plus the other recent homicides, his face reflected horror at the figures set before him now.

"I may as well start with the fellow no one knows," he said, moving around the table, leaning over to inspect what still remained of a once-living man. After much peering and a little probing, he began to speak again.

"All right, now. Anyone can see that death resulted from a close-range shotgun blast, with buckshot—there's a piece, I'd call it double-aught—inflicting lethal damage to the liver, stomach, colon, small intestine, both kidneys, and nearly severing the spine. The good news, if you want to call it that, was that he likely hit the ground unconscious, maybe even dead before the rest of it happened...which was up here."

Wyman had shifted, pointing toward the dead man's throat with shiny forceps from the undertaker's well-stocked tray.

"Here's where one of the creatures, whatever you want to call it, fastened onto him once he was on the ground. Same kind of bite mark to the throat and upper shoulder." Here, his tape measure appeared once more. "And I make this one six-point-five inches across, and call it ten-point-five inches around. Same kind of wound we've seen before, same everything—but wait! This time it left something behind."

The tweezers dipped, rummaged in lifeless flesh, and

came out clutching what Thorn might've taken for a shark's tooth, if he didn't know the killing had been perpetrated on dry land, by something that could fly.

"The hell is that?" asked Marshal Brisbin, seemingly unable to believe his eyes.

"Just what it looks like," Wyman answered. "Not a broken tooth—you see the root, there—but as if it was dislodged by impact from the jaw. As to what *kind* of jaw, all I can do is state the obvious: it doesn't come from any mammal or reptile I've ever seen or read about."

"So, not a bear, then," Brisbin asked.

"Not even close. It still could be mammalian, but...no, sorry, I'm stumped."

Wyman deposited the tooth onto a small plate Grissom offered him, then Othaniel Moore whisked it off to the sink, rinsed it, and dried it with a towel.

"I'd better take that," Brisbin said. "The closest thing we have to evidence so far, even if we can't follow up on it."

"Maybe we can," Thorn said.

"How's that?" the lawman asked.

"If Dr. Müller takes a look at it, he might come up with something from his research."

"Into worms and shrimp, you mean?"

"Unless you have somebody else in mind."

"No. Müller's all we've got, for what he's worth. We haven't got a college in the territory, so I'd have to send it off somewhere, maybe to Texas A.M.C., but like as not I'd never get it back again." Frowning, he took the dried-off tooth from Moore and put it in a pocket of his vest.

By that time, Wyman had moved on to Phil Rutter. "Once more," he said, "it's obvious a gunshot killed this man, but I'm prepared to call it self-inflicted."

"Suicide," Gus Grissom clarified, in case somebody missed the doctor's point.

"Just as you say. He fired the bullet upward through his soft palate into the brain, and I suspect it kept on going when it took the top part of his cranium, shattering both the frontal bone and the parietal. From what I witnessed at the scene, he did that lying down, after he jumped or fell out of the buckboard. Likely saw one of the creatures coming after him and topped himself, as some might say."

"It didn't spare him, though," Brisbin observed.

"Only the pain of being fed on while he lived," Wyman amended. "But you're right. These creatures don't appear to care whether a victim is alive or dead, as long as it's a fresh kill and the blood can be extracted for what I assume is nourishment."

"And we're no closer now to stopping them than when this damned mess started."

No one had a good answer for that, and Brisbin soon excused himself, followed by Dr. Wyman. Thorn followed them out, leaving Grissom and Moore to patch the corpses up as best they could, a long night still ahead of them. No matter how skilled they might be, Gideon guessed closed caskets would be recommended for both men.

And what about the ones who'd disappeared?

"I'm heading back out in the morning," Brisbin said, as if reading Gideon's thoughts. "You wanna help me find those others?"

"If we can."

"Okay, then. See you after breakfast, at the livery. G'night."

Thorn checked his watch against one of Montana Camp's four streetlamps and discovered it was nearly half-past midnight, rolling over into Monday morning. There was still a lamp burning inside the barbershop and Thorn crossed over to it, tried the door, found it unlocked, and went inside.

There was nobody in the shop itself, but yet another of those tinkling bells above the door announced his entry, and a man emerged, bald as a cue ball, dressed up in a shirt and dark trousers under a barber's apron, garters on his sleeves.

"Good evening, friend," he said. "I'm Roland Pike. Welcome to my establishment."

"You're open late," Thorn said.

"Most nights. Some fellas heading home from drinking and the ladies want a trim or shave. Don't ask me why. Maybe the married ones hope that the little missus won't be quite as mad at 'em if they show up smelling of witch hazel, instead of booze or somethin' worse."

"I saw your sign out front. Hot baths?"

"Another late-night favorite. Helps some folks sleep, but I can't say it ever worked for me."

"I'll try one."

"Long day on the trail?"

"And at the undertaker's parlor," Thorn replied.

Pike nodded, as if he'd heard everything before, and didn't press for details. Thorn followed him into a back-room where two large copper tubs stood separated by a half-wall, leaving both sides of the partially divided room accessible.

"Your pick of left or right. Both tubs cleaned out last night and no one's used 'em since."

Thorn veered off to the left, removed his hat and coat, hanging them on wall pegs. Before he got down to essentials, Pike left him alone, then came back with two steaming buckets of water. They filled about one quarter of the tub, and he repeated the procedure twice more while his customer finished undressing. Before stepping into the hot water, Thorn scooted the half-room's single chair within arm's reach and left his gunbelt curled up on its seat.

"I shouldn't be long," he told Pike.

"No skin off me," the barber said. "You get an hour for your twenty cents."

Still dark when Gideon had finished drying off, dressed for the street, and left the shop feeling relaxed, if not entirely clean. He walked back to the Copper Queen, making enough noise to alert the clerk, who stuck his head out of the office, recognized his paying guest, and said, "No messages while you were out, Sir."

Upstairs, Thorn locked himself inside his room and wedged its chair under the doorknob, as if that would keep a flying monster out. Before he got in bed, taking a Colt with him, he checked the window to make sure it was securely latched.

He would allow himself four hours' sleep, grab breakfast at the Mother Lode, and meet Lute Brisbin at the livery as planned, trusting in Shadow to be rested up enough for yet another ride through Bear Valley.

As usual, Thorn was asleep within two minutes after having closed his eyes.

MARCH 5, 1877

Before Thorn and Lute Brisbin reached the scene of last night's massacre, someone had cleared the road. Thorn had already seen Phil Rutter's buckboard, parked beside the livery, and now he saw its two dead horses had been dragged a few yards off, their carcasses mauled by coyotes overnight, now breeding flies.

"I should've had Jake burn 'em," Brisbin said. "I'll have to pay him extra now, to make a second trip."

Thorn was already looking for the blood trails he'd suggested might remain, giving a clue to the direction that the flying predators had come from, or to which they had retreated. He was disappointed by a dearth of bloodstains once he'd searched beyond some thirty feet from where the killings had occurred. If any gore had fallen from bodies carried aloft, he couldn't spot it now, assuming it had soaked into the sand and gravel, or else dried in small drops on the larger stones, resembling weather stains unless he tested each of them in turn with some sensitive chemical he didn't have.

"Well, shit," said Brisbin, when they had been at it for an hour. "It seems to me they're gone."

"And could be anywhere," Thorn grudgingly acknowledged.

"Maybe we could spot 'em from the air, if we searched long enough," Lute said, "but we'd need a hot air balloon, and I'm fresh out."

"At least you haven't lost your sense of humor."

"Easy said. Check back with me on that one when—or *if*—I get an answer from the sheriff's office."

"Nothing yet?"

"Likely as not, Shibell wants to consult the governor before he makes another move. Our Sheriff Charley's big on the consulting—or, as I've been known to say, washing his hands of the responsibility."

Lute's mention of the county sheriff brought Thorn's mind back to the telegram he'd sent out yesterday. "Reminds me that I need to check with Western Union when we get back into town," he said.

"Expecting news?"

"Not really. More like crossing items off a list."

"I've done that and came out with no list left," Brisbin replied.

That sparked another thought. "Still carrying that tooth?" Thorn asked.

"Right here." Brisbin patted the left side of his vest.

"Mind if I borrow it and see what Dr. Müller thinks about it?"

"Be my guest, for all the good that it'll do. Saves me a trip."

Thorn took the tooth, briefly examined it again in sunlight, then stowed it as Brisbin had, in a vest pocket. They parted in Montana Camp, outside the livery, Brisbin going to see his dun stabled and talk to hostler Jake about burning the roadside carcasses. Thorn rode on to the Western Union office, there dismounting, looping Shadow's reins over a hitching post before he went inside.

"Ah, Mr. Thorn," the same clerk greeted him, a tight smile on his face. "I was about to fetch our boy and have him run this telegram to your hotel."

"I might as well just take it now," said Gideon.

"Indeed. This makes the first time I've received a wire from Austria, though not from Europe overall."

Thorn palmed the envelope and took it back outside, leaning against the rail beside Shadow before he opened it. He read the message through, then started over from the top, eyes narrowing. It read:

. . .

SURPRISED BY YOUR INQUIRY, AS I HAVE NOT THOUGHT OF DR. MÜLLER NOW FOR MANY YEARS. WE DIFFERED ON THEORIES AND PARTED COMPANY ON POOR TERMS. CERTAIN MATTERS SHARED IN CONFIDENCE PROHIBIT SAYING MORE BUT I URGE YOU PROCEED WITH CAUTION IN ALL DEALINGS. G. MENDEL.

"What the hell?" Thorn asked himself, and got no answer back from Shadow at his side.

It was approaching lunchtime when Thorn rode back to the *hacienda* occupied by Horst Müller. As on his last visit, the gate stood open and he rode inside, left Shadow in what passed for shade, and mounted low steps to the broad veranda. This time, though, the door opened before he had a chance to knock, and Dr. Müller stood before him, rather than the servant Pablo.

Müller wore a different ensemble than the day before, which seemed entirely natural—brown slacks and vest this time, with a beige shirt—but had retained the bolo tie and gold pince-nez. "Ah, Mr. Thorn," he said. "So soon you come again to see me."

"I apologize for the intrusion, *Señor* Müller."

"It would be *Herr* Müller, by why be so formal? Won't you come in?"

"No, thanks. I only have one question, so I won't monopolize your time."

"So, yes? By all means, ask it, then."

Thorn took the tooth from his vest pocket, held it up between two fingers, watching Müller focus on it through prescriptions lenses that enlarged his moist, gray eyes.

"A tooth, if I am not mistaken?"

"That's correct, Doctor."

"*Ja*, but of what? That is your question, *nein*?"

"It is."

Müller leaned closer, for a better look, then straightened up, frowning. He shook his head. "Alas, I cannot help you there. How did you come by this?"

Thorn laid another of his cards out on the table. "Four more people were attacked last night, not far from here. All dead, as far as we can tell, although we've only found two of the bodies so far."

"*Gott im himmel!* And you found this at the *ort des tötens*? At the killing place?"

"It was extracted from a victim's throat."

"Incredible. You must be on its track, then?"

"Not exactly. I was hoping you could tell me what it came from. If the species isn't clear, perhaps the genus or the family?"

"You are an educated man."

"But not a scientist like you."

"Unfortunately, as I mentioned yesterday, I only work with small species, the annelids, smaller crustaceans, the larval forms of some amphibians. Some of my subjects are no large than this tooth in their entirety."

Thorn nodded. Said, "I thought so, but if I could ask one other question, I'll be on my way."

"Of course."

"If I could contact Dr. Mendel, do you think *he* might be able to identify it from a drawing or a photograph?"

"Mendel?" Müller stuck out his lower lip, perhaps unconsciously, then shook his head. "*Nein, nein.* I doubt that very much. As I explained before, Gregor concerns himself primarily with grafting and mutating flora. That is, plant life, chiefly crops we raise for food."

"Well, it was worth a try. Thanks, anyway. With any luck, I won't intrude on you again."

Thorn pocketed the tooth as Müller said, "*Bitte,* feel free to drop by anytime. Consider my home yours for the duration of your stay."

"That's very generous, and much too kind."

Thorn mounted Shadow, touched his hat brim in farewell, and rode back through the open gate, off toward downtown Montana Camp. As he approached the livery, he spied a small crowd in the street, outside the marshal's office. Veering off in that direction, he reined up a few yards from the mumbling audience while Marshal Brisbin tried to calm them down.

"I've told you all I know for now," Lute said, catching Thorn's eye before he focused on the crowd again. "A miner at the Jayhawk found one of Phil Rutter's men dumped in a gully near the shaft. Couldn't be spotted from the road, apparently, but with a man afoot—"

"What kilt him?" someone called out from Lute's uninvited visitors. "Same thing as all the rest?"

"It looks that way," Brisbin replied. "And no, we still don't know what's doing it."

"Who's 'we'?" a second member of the crowd demanded.

"I've got people looking into it," said Brisbin. "Most of you know Doc Wyman. He's helping out, best as he can, and there are others I'm not free to talk about just now."

Thorn reckoned half the heads in front of him swiveled his way as Brisbin spoke those words. Lute saw it, too, and called out to the worried townsfolk, telling them, "The best thing you can do right now is go about your business, treat this just like any other day."

An angry rumble answered him, but Lute pressed on.

"Like any other day, I said. And when the sun goes down, make sure you're home safe with your loved ones or whoever. Lock your doors and windows. Keep your guns handy but don't go off half-cocked and shoot your neighbors. Leave this to professionals and let us concentrate."

The first man who had spoken up now spat into the dust and jeered, "Fat lotta good your *concentration*'s done so far."

"Nathan," Lute called him out by name, "you're wasting time that could be used tracking the animals that did this. And I say again, they're *animals*, not people. We know that much, anyway, for sure."

The one called Nathan tucked thumbs under his suspenders, rocking on his heels. "But not a bear, I heard you say that, too, and not a cougar. So what *is* it, Marshal? Is you lookin' for a hippy-potty-moose?"

That earned some nervous laughter, but Lute quelled it when he said, "Enough! I don't need to remind you that obstructing criminal investigations is a crime, all on its own. Try it, and you can watch the world go by through bars the next ten days."

Nathan moved off, still blustering and trying to save face, the others scattering to shops and jobs or homes. When they were gone, dispersed along the main street, Gideon edged closer, leaning down and asking Brisbin, "Which one was it?"

"Honestly, I couldn't tell you," Lute replied. "I didn't get a look at what the pair of 'em were wearing yesterday, and now he's got no face to speak of."

"How's that?"

"Damned thing bit his neck as usual, o' course, but when it dropped him—I'd guess forty, fifty feet abouve the ground—he hit headfirst on granite. His own mother wouldn't know 'im now, unless he's got a birthmark hiding somewhere that Doc Wyman didn't look."

"Too bad," Thorn said.

"You got that right. Too bad for him, too bad for us. So, how'd it go with Müller?"

"Nothing doing. Claims he's never seen a tooth like it before, and then told me again he only works on smaller animals like worms and shrimp."

"I note you said he *claims* he can't identify it."

"Well..." After a moment's hesitation, Gideon replied, "I played a hunch and sent a telegram to Müller's old teacher in Austria."

"That Dr. Mengele?"

"Mendel," said Thorn, correcting him.

"Okay. And did he answer you?"

"He did," Thorn said, and handed Lute the telegram. Brisbin unfolded it and read it, top to bottom. "Huh," he said at last. "I guess it's safe to say they're not the best of friends."

"I blew some smoke at Müller, told him I might send Mendel a picture of the tooth Doc Wyman found."

"And?"

"He called it a waste of time. Reminded me that Mendel only studies plants."

"Could be the truth, but I don't like that last bit in his wire: 'I urge you proceed with caution in all dealings'."

Thorn nodded. "The lack of trust is obvious."

"No way to pin it down though, way he talks about those 'certain matters shared in confidence'."

"They definitely had some kind of falling out."

"You know, I never saw the inside of a college," Brisbin said. "Nor hell, the outside of one either. But I hear these academic types get in a snit without much reason for it, feuding over who stole whose brilliant idea, whatever. Maybe go from being friends to back-stabbing each other every chance they get."

"I've seen it for myself," Thorn said. "And that *could* be the trouble, but..."

"But you don't think so."

"Call me undecided," Gideon replied. "If Müller is involved in this somehow, I may have thrown out crumbs enough for him to follow them."

"Which means he'd follow them to you."

"Better than someone else in town, or out there in the countryside."

"But we still don't know he's behind this thing."

"We do not, for a fact," Thorn readily agreed.

"I don't suppose, this time around, you noticed whether he had fangs, or if one of 'em might be missing?"

"Nope. And no wings, either."

"So, we keep on doing it the hard way."

"Until something breaks," Thorn said, "that's all we've got."

ELEVEN

MONTANA CAMP: MARCH 5, 1877

Thorn made another stop at Dr. Wyman's office after leaving Marshal Brisbin and returning Shadow to the livery, spending some time with Belle that Jake the hostler clearly didn't understand. This time, Thorn was surprised to find Wyman engaged in patching up a normal patient, nine or ten years old, a boy who'd fallen down and sprained his wrist while thankfully not breaking it.

After the boy's mother removed him, shooting wary glances at the well-armed visitor in black, Wyman remarked, "You see?? I don't just look at mangled dead folks all day long."

"Must come as a relief," Thorn said.

"Friend, you don't know the half of it. Some days, lately, I feel like packing up and getting out of here for good."

"And leave your patients stranded?"

"That's the hell of it. I'm only here right now because they couldn't get another doctor when they fastened on to me."

"But here you are, counting for something."

"Well, I'd like to think so. But you've come about the other, right?"

"It's like you know me," Thorn replied.

"I'm starting to, I guess. Should I feel sorry for the both of us?"

"Don't ask me that," Gideon answered. "I try not to think about it."

"But you carry on."

"Somebody's got to do it, right?"

"I couldn't answer that for you."

Wyman nodded, then he asked, "You're here about the last one found, I take it."

"If there's anything that you can tell me. I already know from Marshal Brisbin that he wasn't recognizable."

"I could describe the clothes, maybe, if that would help."

Thorn shook his head. "I saw and talked to both of them, briefly, but never got their names."

"I'm stumped, then," said the doctor. "I suppose someone from Mr. Rutter's company should know them."

"Either way, it's not our problem, if they're going back to Tucson," Thorn said. But in truth, he didn't like to think about the dead being forgotten, never mourned by anyone at all.

"So, what's the next move, if you have one?" Wyman asked.

"Seems like it comes down to a waiting game," Thorn said. "Which makes it good for them and bad for us."

The doctor sounded doleful when he said, "As long as anyone on our side lasts."

During Thorn's last stop at the livery, he had advised Shadow that there would be no riding out tonight, unless some unforeseen emergency demanded it. The stallion didn't seem to mind, and Belle, as usual, showed little interest at all.

That didn't mean there'd be no hunting after dark, of course, but Gideon planned doing that alone, on foot, or maybe even from his hotel room. Again, it would depend on what—if anything—transpired after the sun set on Montana Camp.

His next stop, after Wyman's office, was the Mother Lode. Thorn entered to a buzz of conversation that dried up the moment he had crossed the threshold. Several of the faces turned to ogle him were now familiar from the crowd outside of Marshal Brisbin's office earlier, none of them looking friendly in the slightest. Some were frankly hostile, but suspicion seemed to be the ruling order of the day.

The waitress, whom he recognized from earlier, put on a smile that seemed to cost her something, but her tone was relatively jovial, considering what Thorn supposed she must have picked up from her gossipy patrons. A troubled town meant worried people, and he couldn't blame them. Who would be more natural to point a finger at than someone new in town, no matter that they'd seen him working with their marshal to eliminate the threat? The only thing that mattered to most townsfolk at the moment was an absence of results from that attempt. Not knowing who Thorn was—or only having rumors to supply vague details, likely off the mark—simply made matters worse.

He ordered coffee black and read the restaurant's wall-mounted menu, opting for the "chicken fried steak," mashed potatoes with white gravy, peas and carrots on the side. If other diners in the Mother Lode were busy whispering about him while their food got cold, it wasn't Thorn's problem and had no impact on his appetite.

The meal, when it arrived, was ample and delicious. Gideon had tried the entrée previously and enjoyed it well enough to do some basic research on it, learning that the recipe had come across with German immigrants to Texas sometime in the 1830s, filling in for *wiener schnitzel* from their homeland. In the States, beefsteak was generally used in place of veal or pork, coated with seasoned flour and pan-fried. Tonight's was tender, steaming hot, and nicely complemented by its side dishes. Gideon relished it, cleaning his plate and saving room for pecan pie that was so sweet, he asked for a refill on coffee.

While he ate, ignoring his uneasy fellow diners, Thorn recalled his latest talk with Dr. Müller, beginning with the thought that Horst, considering his girth and origin, was probably a fan of *wiener schnitzel* in his own right. Müller's diet, though, was unimportant. Thorn was more concerned about what link—if any—he might have to the ongoing deaths of animals and humans in a bloody ring around Montana Camp.

He'd shown the souvenir of last night's massacre to Müller out of curiosity, to see how he'd react at sight of it, but Thorn had to admit the researcher hadn't betrayed a hint of knowledge as to where it came from or what predatory species might possess such fangs. Even when Thorn had goaded him with Dr. Mendel's name and the suggestion of consulting him, Müller's reaction—although clearly meant to be discouraging—had logically referred to Mendel's scientific focus on plant life, rather than animals.

So...what?

All Thorn had against Müller at the moment was the Mendel telegram, it's warning against trusting Müller, and the reference to matters which a point of confidence forbade Mendel from sharing with a stranger overseas. That could mean anything, and Lute Brisbin was accurate in his assessment of some university professors, their ability to harbor long-term grudges over things that meant nothing to a majority of men and women in their daily lives.

At Harvard, there'd been two professors in the History Department who'd despised each other, solely based on their divergent theories of mankind's origins. One reckoned southern Africa had been the birthplace of humanity; the other was convinced the cradle of Earth's first crude men and women lay somewhere in region French imperialists labeled Indo-China. From that starting point of academic disagreement, the two scholars had gone on to snub each other socially, indulged in character assassination, and at last had come to blows, placing both men in danger of suspension from the faculty.

Thorn had nothing so far to suggest that matters had degenerated to that point between Mendel and Müller, even when he'd given Müller opportunity to bad-mouth Mendel personally. Simply stating that his old professor limited research to flora versus fauna didn't rank as an insult, and even that was tempered by Müller's remark that Mendel focused mainly on improving crops to better feed a hungry world—a compliment of sorts

Gideon couldn't make a feud of that. If anything, Mendel had cast aspersions on his former student, while eliciting no anger in return. Of course, he hadn't shown Müller the telegram from Austria. There'd been no call for introducing it, and Thorn had feared tipping his hand, in case...of what?

The only thing he had so far was vague suspicion, not

unlike what diners at the Mother Lode had shown toward him. It might turn out to be a wild-goose chase, a total waste of time.

And yet...

Thorn paid his tab and left the restaurant, pausing to frown and cock one eyebrow at a couple seated near the door, so wrapped up in observing him and whispering that they had nearly left their meals untouched. He recognized a sense of almost childish pleasure when they flinched and dropped their eyes, pretending to enjoy their tepid food, and fought an urge to whistle as he left the restaurant.

Back at the Copper Queen, Thorn went upstairs, secured his door as usual, and set about preparing for a night on watch. He didn't have a clue how one or more of the nocturnal predators might find him, knowing as he did that they'd never attacked within Montana Camp's town limits, but he didn't mean to throw his life away on a long shot by letting down his guard.

Thorn started with his Sharps, slipping a .50-90 round into the rifle's single-shot chamber. The designation meant each cartridge packed a .50-caliber greased-groove projectile weighing close to fifteen ounces, powered by ninety grains of black powder. Each bullet left the weapon's muzzle at approximately 1,800 feet per second, striking with some 3,000 foot-pounds of catastrophic energy.

The drawback was reloading after each shot, though a practiced rifleman like Gideon could manage eight to ten rounds in one minute if he kept his wits about him under fire. The rifle's special scope, alas, could work against him for night shooting, when he might have only seconds to acquire a flying target and take aim.

For rapid fire, on point in an emergency, Thorn would rely on his Winchester rifle and twin Colts. The three firearms combined allowed him twenty-eight shots before having to reload, each round loaded with forty grains of powder, driving a .44-caliber, fourteen-gram slug down range at some 1,245 feet per second, hammering a target—if he hit it—with 688 foot-pounds of energy.

No man could stand before that concentrated fire. As for a larger animal...well, Thorn would have to wait and see, given the chance.

All useless to him in his hotel room, granted, unless the winged killers who'd been terrorizing local folk elected to invade Montana Camp for once and give Thorn his first opportunity to drop one from the sky.

He didn't like the odds against him, but since prowling through the countryside by night had failed, he hoped the changeup might produce results.

Seated on the bed, surrounded by his guns and with his window open on the night, Thorn settled back to wait.

"I'll make the first round," Lute Brisbin informed his deputy, "and we can switch off after that. One of us needs some shut-eye, I've tried out the cots in both cells and they're not half bad."

Both cells were empty at the moment, and Lute hoped they stayed that way.

"I still say you should go on home like usual," Win Cowan answered. "It's a Monday night, and nothin' much happens at the saloons. If somethin' does, I've handled it before. Worse come to worst, you're just a couple blocks away."

"I know all that," the marshal said. "And *you* know I'm not thinking about drunks."

"I get it," Win replied. "You're worried about *them,* but all this time, they've never come in town. Not once."

"We don't know that," Lute said. "We've never *seen* 'em, and they haven't *killed* in town so far. That doesn't mean none of 'em's come and had a look around."

"And doesn't mean they *have,* neither," Win fired right back. "This Rutter business has you more het up than usual."

"And that's the problem," Brisbin said, "right there. These killing shouldn't be 'the usual.' I'm surprised we haven't caught hell over Rutter and his men already, but I feel it coming, whether it's tomorrow or the next day. When it hits, I won't have Sheriff Charley or the governor saying I let our people down by going home to sleep."

"Okay, you win," said Cowan. "Both of us stay up all night and go around to rattle doors by turns. But if you have to prop your eyes open with toothpicks in the morning, don't blame me."

"You're blameless," Brisbin said, before he closed the office door behind him, starting on his rounds. It felt peculiar, carrying the sawed-off shotgun that they kept around in case some kind of riot broke out in Montana Camp, but Lute drew reassurance from its weight in hand as he set off along the wooden sidewalk, passing in and out of light between the town's quartet of widely spaced streetlamps.

All the shops and offices were dark and shut up tight, except his own spot at the local jail. The only other signs of life past dusk came from Montana Camp's saloons, and from the sound of it, even their nightly trade was minimal. Lute wasn't a teetotaler and didn't like to see their business suffer, even though he'd never personally liked the thought of whores humping away upstairs, but in the midst of crisis, everybody felt the pinch somehow.

For ranchers in Bear Valley's countryside, it meant long, yawning vigils after sundown, trying to protect loved ones and livestock, the dark hours running into weary days when lack of sleep bred accidents, forgetfulness, and short tempers. For merchants, it meant fewer customers out and about, most residents sticking closer to home unless they were required at paying jobs or had to stock up on necessities. To miners, it meant adding fear of vicious fangs to all the other dangers they faced underground, including cave-ins, toxic gas, and worry that a vein might peter out and take away their jobs.

Brisbin approached the Dry Gulch first, peering through streetside windows, pausing to look over batwing doors. The joint's piano player banged out tunes from memory or improvised if he forgot which notes came next, but Lute only counted nine drinkers at the bar, nobody playing cards. He guessed a couple more might be upstairs, rattling headboards in the cribs, but the one "hostess" he saw at work could barely dredge up energy enough to cadge a drink.

Hard times for bartenders and pimps, as well, since winged death began to prowl by night.

The only business in town that seemed to profit from their plague in progress was the Baptist church, domain of Reverend Ellwood Belcher and his Sunday invocations of hellfire. Lute thought of preaching as a business, since he'd never seen it come without a price attached from tithes and offerings. Shortly after the killings started, Belcher had begun holding more services on Wednesday nights, which he called "vespers," and while no one was explicitly compelled to purchase pew time, all those who attended knew the minister expected some expression of largesse.

And if Belcher implied that prayers carried more weight

with cash money behind them...well, that wasn't criminal, just showmanship.

Tonight, the church was dark and silent, so Lute moved on to the next saloon in line. That was the Lucky Strike, whose owner hadn't stuck much luck tonight. Looking inside as he passed by, Brisbin noted three men playing a game of poker without much enthusiasm evident, a not-so-fancy woman watching them, and half a dozen solitary customers spaced out along the bar.

No trouble there, except for the proprietor watching his profits fade, so Lute moved on.

The Gold Dust was his last saloon before he made a quick swing past the Copper Queen, then back to his office. Looking inside, Lute saw one of the whores—Inez? Irene? What did it matter?—leading some young guy upstairs who looked to be a miner. Otherwise, the barroom had six customers with desultory faces, and the one en route to get his ashes hauled didn't seem all that pleased about it, either.

Turning toward the Copper Queen, he saw a lighted window at the northwest corner of the hotel's second floor. Would that be Thorn's? The only other light showing inside was from the lobby, dim enough to indicate a lamp inside the manager's office, behind the registration desk.

A quick peek, then I'm done, the lawman told himself, and stepped into the street. A second later, he stopped dead, arrested in mid-stride.

Whop-whop!

"The hell was that?" Lute asked aloud, with no one anywhere around to answer him. He looked along the town's main street, first north, then south, but saw nothing that would explain the sound.

Whop-whop-whop!

Turning back the way he'd come, the marshal faced a pitch-black alley that ran east to west along the north side of the Gold Dust. He thumbed back his shotgun's twin hammers and took a long stride toward the alley's mouth, heart in his throat, but not about to let fear of the unknown hobble him.

Or was it fear of what he *knew,* a grisly death inflicted by a wide mouth filled with fangs?

Lute held the twelve-gauge pointed forward, stock clutched tight between his elbow and his hip in case he had to fire without aiming. Not that he needed to, with this gun. Just consider what Phil Rutter's scattergun had done to his unlucky driver last night, when they met disaster on the road.

"You best come out of there right now," he warned the alley's shadows, "with your hands high up where I can see 'em empty. Try me on tonight and you'll be going home in pieces, whoever you are."

"It's *me*, Marshal!"

"Who's 'me'?"

"Dean! You known me for a long time."

"Dean Postlewaite?"

"Who else? You seen me just last night."

The damned town drunk, Lute thought.

"What are you doing back there, then?"

"Takin' a leak is all. I knowed I'd never make it home."

"All right. Come out then, like I told you."

"I just need a sec to button up my fly before I—"

"Never mind that, damn you! Come out *now*!"

"Okay, Marshal. I'm comin'. Just go easy with that scattergun."

Dean lurched into the faint lamplight, hands raised around the level of his narrow shoulders, fly gaping below.

Brisbin exhaled a pent-up breath and told him, "Put that little worm of yours away before somebody runs a fishhook through it."

"Tha's a good one, that is, Marshal. Always like a joke, myself. Joke and a drink, ya know what I—"

Whop-whop-whop-whop!

This time the sound came from Lute's left. He turned his head in that direction, still covering Dean with his sawed-off. For a heartbeat, he imagined that the night had been made flesh and it was hurtling toward him, close to twenty feet across, seeming ephemeral until it struck him like a charging bronco, sweeping Brisbin off his feet.

Dean shrieked, and Brisbin heard the twelve-gauge fire both barrels, unaware of doing it himself. Away off to his right, as he was falling, he heard glass shatter and something falling on the far side of the shop window he'd blown to brittle shards. Then he was screaming with his chest afire from talons ripping into it, and that was all that he would ever hear again.

In his hotel room, with the window open and a night breeze ruffling the curtain, Thorn heard shouting from the street below, then leathery flapping, a shotgun blast that cleared out the display window of Fletcher's millinery shop, and finally a man's hoarse scream.

No, make that two screams, one more high-pitched than the other, with the deeper voice quickly cut off and smothered.

Gideon was at the window by that time and looking down into the street. He saw a kind of animated shadow bowl over the marshal, wings enfolding him, a dark head ducking toward his face or throat. Raising his Sharps, Thorn aimed as quickly as he could, allowing for the barrel-mounted telescope that measured more than two feet long, afraid of hitting Brisbin if he fired into the center of the struggling, twisting mass below.

He pulled the shot a bit off to the left and squeezed the rifle's trigger, riding out its recoil before peering through the gunsmoke cloud to mark his hit. The beast had peeled away from Brisbin's supine form, rising, its left wing obviously injured as it rushed a second man on the sidewalk, down on his knees with arms folded over his head, and hurtled past him toward an alleyway, passing him by with mere inches to spare.

His rifle shot still echoing along the street, Thorn tossed his Sharps onto the bed, snatched up his Winchester, and bolted from the room, sparing seconds to lock the door behind him with his hotel key. He vaulted down the stairs, four at a time, and passed the registration desk at top speed, heard the clerk call after him, "Was that a shot?"

Ignoring him, Thorn reached the street and ran toward where Lute Brisbin lay spread-eagle in the dust, dark blood pumping from his torn throat. Win Cowan reached his boss first, covering a shorter distance from the marshal's office, while the man whom Gideon recalled as "Dean" knelt by the alley's mouth, babbling.

"It ain't my fault!" the drunkard wailed. "I never touched 'im! Swear to God I never laid a finger on 'im!"

"Shut your mouth and fetch Doc Wyman," Brisbin's deputy commanded, and when Dean was slow to move, added, "Go on, before I plug you one!"

Dean struggled to his feet, his penis flopping from an open fly, and started off toward Wyman's office at a shambling run, while Cowan knelt beside the marshal, dropped his pistol in the dirt, and clapped both hands over Lute Brisbin's spurting wound.

Thorn could've told Win that he was too late, too much blood spilled or otherwise extracted by the time they reached the dying man, but he left Cowan to it, telling him, "It flew off down the alley."

"Kill the sumbitch!" Cowan snapped at him, without raising his head.

Gideon moved to stand before the alley's mouth—nothing but darkness onward from that point—and listened for a second, ears alert for any sound of movement. There was faint light from starshine down at the alley's other end, and he pursued it with his head tucked down to guard his throat, a death grip on his Winchester.

Nothing sprang out to tackle Thorn along the way. Nothing obstructed him except some scattered garbage underfoot, and he kicked that aside. If anything was waiting for him at the alley's far end, it was bound to hear him coming, given ample time to lie in wait and ambush him.

But he wouldn't go down without a fight.

He owed that much to Brisbin and the people of Montana Camp.

And when Thorn reached his destination, facing on to houses built behind the main street's shops, he found—nothing.

Some lamps were coming on in scattered windows, up and down the secondary street, but there was no sign of the creature that had done for Lute. Thorn glanced about for signs of spattered blood, but there were no street lamps beyond Montana Camp's main street, and he would have to wait for sunrise to conduct a search.

Cursing, Thorn doubled back and didn't mind his step

on the return jog, stepping from the alley's mouth in half the time he'd spent clearing its length. Off to his left, he saw Doc Wyman coming on the run, bag gripped in one hand, with the man called Dean trailing behind him, buttoning his fly at last.

And in the street, Win Cowan had leaned back away from Marshal Brisbin, bloodstained hands smearing his trousers where they rested on his thighs. He didn't seem to notice Thorn, but saw the doctor loping toward him.

"May as well slow down, Doc," he called out to Wyman. "Lute's gone. All of us were too damned late."

TWELVE

MARCH 6, 1877

Montana Camp had no "Boot Hill," per se. Its cemetery was a patch of desert situated south of town, along the road that travelers leaving the States could follow to Old Mexico. Wildflowers plucked to decorate some of the recent graves had withered and lay dead before wooden grave markers, under the relentless sun.

At ten minutes to noon on Tuesday, some two hundred people turned out for Lute Brisbin's burial. He'd never mentioned living family to anyone in town, so there'd been no one to alert, no one to speculate about the ex-lawman's last wishes.

If he'd been asked, Thorn might've guessed that Brisbin's parting thought was something in the line of "Get this goddamned monster off of me."

He'd managed that with one round from his Sharps, but by the time he'd triggered it, the marshal was already beyond any help. Doc Wyman had confirmed that both Lute's jugular and his carotid artery were severed on the right side, by his slayer's teeth, the blood exploding out of him and down the creature's gullet until Thorn's slug drove it off. From that point, any still remaining to the marshal either soaked into his clothes or stained the dusty thoroughfare where he had fallen. It was a rotten way to die, Wyman opined, but relatively swift.

He wouldn't vouch for painless, though.

A preacher Thorn had yet to see around Montana Camp officiated at the burying. Win Cowan had confirmed Thorn's supposition that the minister was Ellwood Belcher, pastor of the town's sole church. Business beneath its spire was booming lately, with the killings, Cowan granted, but once the elusive predators were finally killed off—assuming that they ever were—he reckoned that most of the townsfolk would go back to sleeping in on Sunday mornings as they had before.

Cowan was acting marshal of Montana Camp for now, till someone higher up the ladder of authority either confirmed or fired him. As it was, he didn't seem to care much, either way. Any commitment to the law he might've felt while serving as Lute Brisbin's deputy was now submerged, his top priority being revenge.

"The marshal always done right by me," he'd explained, after Thorn and some others helped him carry Brisbin to the undertaker's parlor. "Seems to me I let him down there, at the end. I ain't forgettin' that. I'm gonna make it right."

Implicit in his words were Cowan's sense that Thorn had likewise failed the late lawman. Gideon didn't see it that way, not exactly, reasoning that anybody on the street last night—the drunken Dean, for instance—would've been acceptable as prey.

An idle thought: Would drinking Dean have made the creature tipsy? And who even cared?

Thorn knew he'd done his best to help Brisbin, once the attack began. Before that, he couldn't have stopped the marshal from patrolling overnight, and would've been rebuffed if he had tried it. Cowan's guilt, Thorn knew, derived at least in part from having failed to talk his boss out of the extra duty, leaving the patrols to him. In which case, it would be his corpse inside the pale pine box, or maybe drunken Dean's.

Gideon didn't feel like trying to decide which death would have been least traumatic for Montana Camp. Beyond a certain point, he knew, the horrors ran together and a person's mind went numb—if they were lucky, anyway.

If not, they'd likely go insane.

After a final prayer from Belcher and a ragged chorus of "amens," Thorn left the cemetery with Win Cowan and the plump redhead who'd come along with him, identified simply as Cherry, walking back through noonday heat to reach the marshal's office. Cherry left them there, while Thorn and Cowan went inside. Win sank into the swivel chair behind his predecessor's desk, while Thorn stood, scanning WANTED notices tacked up on a corkboard.

"So, the blood led nowhere," Cowan said.

He knew the answer, wasn't really asking, but his comment served to break the awkward silence.

Earlier that morning, shortly after sunrise, Thorn had gone back to the alley he'd traversed last night, seeking traces of whatever it was he'd wounded with his Sharps. From the creature's clumsy takeoff afterward, Thorn knew he hadn't missed entirely, literally winging it, and he'd found blood speckling the alley's length by daylight. Whatever it was had paused briefly at the far end and bled a little more, then took wing, probably in pain, and flapped away to God knew where. If any further blood had fallen as it fled, Thorn guessed he'd have to search rooftops and rummage through mesquite to find its traces, likely leading nowhere.

"Anyway," said Cowan, "I come up with an idea."

"Which is?"

"Josiah Walker."

"Who's that?"

"Best tracker in this part of the territory, far as I know. He's a Papago, or Tohono O'odham, whatever. Lives out on the rez but comes in town sometimes and hires out, showin' hunters down from Tucson, even Phoenix, where to look for game."

"You're thinking he could help us find these things we're after?"

"I ain't sure, but what else have we got?"

Gideon thought of Dr. Müller and considered briefing Win on what he'd told Lute Brisbin, but instead replied, "You're right. It couldn't hurt."

"Besides," Win said, "the marshal wanted to find out if there'd been any killin's on the rez, but never got around to it."

"Well, you're the marshal now," Thorn told him.

"Right. Ain't sure I'm up to it, but what the hell. Long as I got the badge, I aim to use it."

"So, when did you want to leave?"

"Soon as I get something to eat," Win said. "I plumb forgot breakfast, and now my belly's growlin' like a catamount."

"Same here. You pick, between the restaurants. The meal's on me."

They wound up going to Delmonico's, ordered steak with eggs and fried potatoes on the side, washed down with black coffee to ward off any drowsiness from interrupted sleep last night. From there, Thorn went back to the Copper Queen and fetched both of his rifles, passed the day shift clerk on his way out, and met Win Cowan at the livery.

Shadow knew Thorn was coming, seeming anxious to be out and on the hunt. Belle didn't mind staying behind, munching her feed and listening to whatever the stable's horses had to say.

Cowan arrived armed with a Yellow Boy Winchester, in addition to his sidearm, and watched Jake the hostler finish saddling his animal, a palomino mare. Leaving Montana Camp, they rode north past the working mines—each one with posted guards on hand today—and past the recent ambush site, where the dead horses from Phil Rutter's buckboard had been doused with kerosene and burned.

In Thorn's opinion, while the fire had done for maggots and the like, the smell it left behind was no improvement over dead meat rotting in the sun. The blaze hadn't been kept up long enough to leave only the skeletons behind, although the two horses resembled blackened mummies now, instead of bloating up like leather gas balloons.

A mile or so beyond the slaughter ground, the road forked—something Gideon had overlooked as he'd approached Montana Camp, only four days ago. He followed Cowan's lead onto the left-hand track, presumably conveying them onto the reservation, or at least one corner of its 4,400-square-mile area. Ten minutes later, they rode past a professionally painted sign advising them that they were leaving Pima County's legal jurisdiction, entering restricted property of the United States.

"Don't mind that," Cowan told him, as they left the

warning sign behind. "The redskins know me purty well out here."

"You might not want to call them that," suggested Gideon.

"My mama didn't raise no fools," Cowan replied.

After they'd ridden for another half-mile, more or less, four long-haired riders met them on the road, waiting atop a rise for Thorn and Cowan to approach. All four were armed: two packing Sharps carbines, a model used by cavalry on both sides of the U.S. Civil War; one with a Model 1866 Winchester Yellow Boy like Cowan's; their apparent leader with a Colt Dragoon Revolver, also dating from the Civil War, tucked underneath a sash he'd tied around his waist.

The pistol-packer was the one who spoke up first, asking Cowan, "You lost, Deputy Win?"

"I don't get lost, Red Eagle," Cowan answered. "And it's acting marshal for a little while, at least."

"What happened to the other marshal, then?"

Win kept it short. "Got killed last night. I'm hopin' you can help me us out with that."

"Who is the other half of 'us'?" Red Eagle asked.

Thorn answered for himself, stating his name and tacking on, "The marshal—*late* marshal—asked me to help him with some killings they've had going on around Montana Camp of late."

Turning away from Thorn, Red Eagle asked, "What makes you think that we can help you, Marshal Win?"

"Not you, exactly," Cowan said. "Josiah Walker."

"Does he know you're coming for him?"

"He'll know when I tell him."

"If you plan arresting him—"

"I don't have the authority. Heard it before."

"Ah. So, you wish his help to hunt a killer, then?"

"I'm told there's more than one, but they ain't human."

"No?" The three riders with Red Eagle were trading glances, shifting slightly on their mounts. "What, then?"

"Somethin' that flies by night, kills people and their livestock, drinks most of the blood. I also had in mind to ask if you've had any troubles like that out here, on the rez."

"We don't discuss these things with white eyes," said Red Eagle. "But if you sit down with Spotted Wolf and tell your story, he might help you, if our law permits it."

"Guess we'd better go and see him, then."

"Keep your guns for now, and follow me."

Red Eagle turned his horse around, his three companions fading back as Thorn and Cowan followed, moving in behind them so the white men couldn't change their mind and try to flee.

"Who's Spotted Wolf?"" Thorn asked Cowan, not bothering to whisper in the circumstances.

"He's their chief or holy man, I disremember which it is,"

"Both," said Red Eagle without turning to face them. "You will show him respect."

"No doubt about it," Win replied, raising an eyebrow only Thorn could see.

They traveled in formation for another half-hour, the afternoon advancing, till they reached a settlement where tipis stood beside frame houses, cook fires burning in the open under clear blue sky. The central feature of the village was a longhouse built of logs, spacious enough to fit a quartet of the smaller dwellings underneath its sloping roof. Thorn guessed it was the home of Spotted Owl, or maybe his administration center for the reservation. At the door, two Indian policemen dressed in U.S. Cavalry jackets without the usual insignia, worn over buckskin pants and moccasins, watched the procession draw abreast of them and halt.

Red Eagle told something in a language new to Gideon, presumably the native tongue of the Tohono O'odham people. One policeman nodded, ducked inside the longhouse, while the other moved to block the entryway, eyeing the white interlopers with a thinly veiled hostility.

The first cop reappeared a moment later, said something to Red Eagle, and he in turn spoke English, saying, "I will take you in to Spotted Wolf now. Leave your rifles in their scabbards. Keep the pistols if you like."

As if we'd dare to use them, Gideon mused silently. At least a hundred tribespeople had gathered in the front yard of the longhouse by this time, and while most of them were unarmed, he counted four more rifles in the mix, along with eight or nine men wearing knives that he could see. From the expressions on their faces, most of them would welcome an excuse to strike.

Thorn wasn't sure what to expect, maybe a throne atop a dais for the tribal chief and holy man or shaman, rolled up into one. What he beheld, instead, when ushered into Spotted Wolf's presence, was what appeared to be an army surplus desk and straight-backed wooden chair he thought looked none too comfortable. In said chair, an old man sat, gray hair tied back into a ponytail above a plaid shirt buttoned to the collar with no tie, under a vest that had been decorated with elaborate beadwork.

The chief seemed ageless beyond obviously being old. Based on his deeply lined bronze face, he might have been somewhere in his mid-sixties, or perhaps two decades older. When he spoke, before Red Eagle had a chance to introduce the visitors, his voice sounded a bit like water rippling over gravel in a desert stream.

"The white men, finally," he said. "I've been expecting you."

Red Eagle tried to brief him, starting out, "Wise One, they've come to—"

Spotted Wolf silenced his minion with a look, not even bothering to raise a hand. "I know all that," he said. "The question must be why they waited until now." His eyes bored into Thorn and Cowan, each in turn, as he ordered, "Bring chairs, then leave us."

"But—"

This time, the chief did lift a calloused warning hand. "Enough. These men are capable of speech. Two chairs. Now. Then leave us alone."

Glaring at the white visitors, clearly afraid of talking back, Red Eagle fetched two more plain chairs that Gideon had overlooked, tucked in a corner near the meeting chamber's entryway, then hurried from the room.

Win Cowan tried to start his pitch. "We come out here to ask—"

"First, let me tell you what I know. Your settlement has suffered deaths, both animals and human beings, eh? I feel...ten people dead, is it? Most recently your marshal fell, who has consulted with me several times. Now you replace him, yes?"

"That's right." Win's voice was hushed. Clearly, he had been taken by surprise. "I had in mind to ask if your people have dealt with anything like that of late."

"No members of our nation have been lost, as yet," the chief replied. "But animals, oh yes. Two horses, half a dozen cattle we could not afford to lose, and sheep. I make their number nine."

Nodding toward Thorn, Win said, "We mean to stop that, if we can."

"This one," said Spotted Wolf, now facing Gideon directly. "He is marked, yes?"

Thorn removed his hat and ducked his head, giving the chief a clear view of the white blaze on his scalp. "From childhood," he replied. "A claw did that. The same thing killed my parents and my brother."

"But you've settled that," said Spotted Wolf, "Or *hope* you have."

Gideon didn't like the sound of that but let it go. "I've been around some, seen some things my own people would laugh at if I tried to tell it straight."

"You'll meet no laughter here, White Hair. We, the Tohono O'odham, recognize a world—or more than one—beyond what others understand and teach through their religions when they are deemed 'civilized'."

"That's one thing I admire about your people," Thorn replied.

"You have confronted the winged death, yes? Very recently?"

"Last night," said Gideon. "I wounded it but couldn't bring it down. The doctor in Montana Camp's examined evidence that makes him think there's more than one creature involved."

"Indeed. He speaks wisdom."

Cowan broke into their dialogue, saying, "We rode out here hoping Josiah Walker might could help us track the damned things down someway."

"Josiah's skills are far advanced. You may not realize the half of it."

"Sounds like the very man we need," Win said.

"But even he, I fear, can't track a shadow on the wing."

"So, we can't hire him, then?"

"Of course you may, if he is willing," Spotted Wolf replied. "But you should not expect him to work miracles."

"I've long since given up on those," the acting marshal answered.

"And perhaps the time has come for you to reconsider that," said Spotted Wolf. "But never mind. I'm not your shaman or your 'pastor,' as the white men call it."

"Not real big on church, either," Win said.

"But *you,*" the shaman aimed an index finger toward Gideon. "You have sampled and accepted portions of many beliefs, I see."

A chill passed down Thorn's spine before he reached up to his neck and brought the silver necklace out, festooned with icons of disparate faiths. "I take what I think I can use," he said, "and leave the rest behind."

"Wisdom," said Spotted Wolf, nodding. "Do you feel the wings of death around you?"

"Not right now," Thorn said. "But I came close last night."

"I'm speaking of the future, not your past."

"Sadly, that's closed to me."

"Not all men have the sight, but you have...something else, I think, to do with animals."

Thorn felt Win staring at him now and shrugged. Replied to Spotted Wolf, "It's hit-and-miss. Sometimes I get a glimmer, other times, nothing."

The chief nodded again. "Before you put your question to Josiah," he said, "you will stay and share a meal with us."

"Chief, I'm afraid it'll be dark soon," Cowan said.

"And you are right to be afraid, Marshal. But here is where a portion of your answer lies. It comes to you unbidden, with the night."

"And it'll be dark pretty soon, Chief."

"It will come no matter where you are. As to this man you seek..."

"Man?" Cowan glanced from Spotted Wolf to Thorn and back again. "Which man is that?"

Thorn hadn't mentioned Gregor Mendel's telegram after Lute Brisbin's death, for fear the deputy might take some action that would land him in his own lockup. Now, it was clear to him that Brisbin hadn't shared the information with his deputy, either.

Thorn said to Spotted Wolf, "I don't have any evidence against him. Nothing even close."

"But that is for your courts of law, yes?" Reaching up to tap his own chest, Spotted Wolf went on. "You feel something...in here."

"What *man*?" Cowan demanded once again. "Somebody spill the beans, will ya?"

Addressing him, the shaman said, "He is a member of your race but not your nation. As of now, his reasons—what your lawyers call *motives*—are still unknown to me. Still, he knows what these creatures are and why they hunt. He is their father."

"Huh?" Win was beyond confusion now. "How can a *man* be father to these monsters? They ain't any part of human."

Spotted Wolf reached up this time to tap his cranium. "Creation starts here, Marshal. It need not involve the loins."

Cowan had swiveled in his chair, now facing Gideon. "We're gonna have this out, Mister, as soon as we get outa here."

"Not yet," said Spotted Wolf. "You must remain and share a meal with us, and only then—"

The door burst open, slamming back against the nearest well. Three pairs of eyes pinned Red Eagle standing on the threshold, with his Colt Dragoon in hand. "Chief, you must come with me!" he blurted out. "The monsters—"

"I know where my place is," Spotted Wolf replied, and got up nimbly for a man his age, whatever that might be. Before Cowan and Thorn were on their feet, the chief was halfway to the exit, with Red Eagle trailing after him, protesting all the way.

"Chief, you must follow me to safety now."

"And where is that?" the shaman answered without slowing down or turning. "You know that no one is safe while these monsters draw breath."

"But—"

Thorn and Cowan caught up with the others as they cleared the longhouse, Gideon a bit surprised to find that dusk had fallen while they were inside with Spotted Wolf. He had lost track of time in there, and now he scanned the nearly dark sky overhead, counting three shadows as they circled almost lazily. One of them screeched, evoking answers from the other two.

He stepped to Shadow, drew his Winchester out of its saddle boot, as Cowan reached his palomino and unsheathed his Yellow Boy. Thorn didn't want to waste his ammunition on targets that were, if not beyond effective range, at least bobbing and weaving, swooping low, then rising up again, without a seeming pattern to their movements.

Cowan didn't let that stop him, squeezing off one of his weapon's rimfire .44-caliber Henry bullets. No sooner had his rifle barked, than several of the armed Tohono O'odham men fired off their Sharps carbines into the sky, their .45-70 Government rounds eclipsing Cowan's smaller caliber.

And still Thorn waited for a shot that wouldn't simply be a waste of lead.

Off to his left, Red Eagle stood in front of Spotted Wolf, his pistol—nearly fifteen inches long—raised like a talisman against the night. Thorn heard the chief, their shaman, chanting something in his native tongue, hands raised and empty as if summoning some otherworldly power from on high.

Silently wishing him good luck, Thorn saw one of the creatures plummet toward the chief, keening like claws on slate, setting his teeth on edge. Before he had a chance to fire his Winchester, Red Eagle interposed himself between the swooping thing and Spotted Wolf, firing two .44 rounds from his Colt Dragoon before it struck him, clamping down with clawed hind feet and spinning him away.

Thorn fired then, had to try it, and he saw the great winged creature—so much like the bats he was familiar with, but vastly larger—lurch and wobble as his shot struck home. It dropped Red Eagle first, the warrior yelping as he tumbled fifteen feet or more and hit the ground, then fell to land a few yards distant from him as Red Eagle staggered to his feet.

The warrior fired repeatedly into his would-be killer's body, emptying his Colt, and by the time he'd spent those six rounds, other tribesmen joined him, blasting at it with their single-shot carbines, each stepping back to reload after he had fired. One braved the storm of lead to strike the dying monster's skull with the blade of a tomahawk.

Above the milling earthbound group that sparked with muzzle flashes, marksmen's eyesight dimmed by drifting gunsmoke, the remaining creatures shrieked in what, to Thorn, sounded like bitter rage. Rising, they twirled like giant leaves above a roaring bonfire, rising on a draft of heated air. Within seconds, as suddenly as they'd appeared, the creatures vanished, black on black, stars flickering behind them as the great wings blocked them out, and then moved on.

Thorn looked around the battlefield and saw one Tohono O'odham woman lying in blood, others weeping above her, while a sobbing child knelt at her side. Somehow, during the confrontation's chaos, one of the attackers must have swept down on her, ripped her slender throat open with fangs or claws, and then retreated from the hammering gunfire, leaving its prey behind.

Around the yard, Thorn saw two other tribesmen being tended for flesh wounds that likely would prove minor, if the creatures were not venomous or carrying disease. Some bats, he'd heard, were prone to bearing rabies, though he'd never personally seen one on his travels through the West.

As for venom, even without detailed examination Thorn could tell the dead thing being hacked and stabbed by vengeful tribe members must be a mammal of some species presently unclassified. Thorn's studies in zoology at Harvard told him that venomous mammals, thankfully, were few and far between: three shrew species, scattered around the globe from North America to the Near East; a shrew-like creature known as a solenodon, restricted to a few islands in the Caribbean; and from Australia, the peculiar duck-billed platypus, whose males had claws with venom glands in their hind feet.

As for the creatures he'd been hunting lately, Thorn was certain nothing like them had been catalogued or written up in textbooks.

"Sons of bitches," Cowan said, approaching him. "It's like the damned things waited for us, knowin' we'd be here."

"I wouldn't give them too much credit," Thorn replied.

"Oh, no? Speakin' of credit, were you ever gonna tip me to your lead about some man behind all this?"

"It's not a lead," Thorn said, then felt compelled to add, "not really. Marshal Brisbin would've told you, if he'd thought it might pan out."

"You may have noticed that he's *dead*." Win fairly spat the words at Thorn. "Now, are you gonna give, or not?"

Before Gideon could reply, a tribesman stepped in close to them, holding a rifle in one hand, its muzzle pointed at the ground. "I understand you're looking for me," he declared.

"And who are you?" Cowan replied.

"Josiah Walker, at your service."

THIRTEEN

The ride back to Montana Camp was tense and silent for the most part. None of the three horsemen craved distraction with their airborne enemies abroad and seeking prey. Among the three, Josiah Walker was the odd man out, barely acquainted with Win Cowan and a total stranger to Gideon Thorn.

Gideon guessed that Walker was somewhere in his mid-thirties, hair cut shorter than the other tribesmen he'd seen on the reservation, stocky, clad in buckskin from his laced-up tunic to his knee-high moccasins. His long gun was a Colt revolving rifle chambered for .44-caliber rounds, and on his belt he wore a Colt Navy revolver holstered for a cross-hand draw, leaving his right hip to support a hunting knife.

Before leaving the reservation, Cowan had arranged with Spotted Wolf for someone from Montana Camp to call next morning, hauling off the creature they had killed. Until then, tribesmen planned to keep it under guard against nocturnal scavengers, and Spotted Wolf had indicated that he planned a cleansing ritual to exorcise the monster's evil spirit.

Thorn, for his part, recognized the dead thing as a flesh-and-blood monstrosity, most like a bat in overall appearance, if those small and harmless insect-eaters were inflated ten to fifteen times their normal size. He'd also pried the creature's lips back with his Bowie's blade and recognized teeth like the one recovered from the Rutter ambush site last night.

Arriving in Montana Camp, the riders stopped first at the livery, where Thorn paid Jake the hostler to take care of Walker's chestnut stallion. Once the animals had been unsaddled and were safely in their stalls, the three walked back to Cowan's office, with the marshal steaming but apparently inhibited by Walker joining them.

When they were shut inside the office, Win could hold his tongue no longer. Facing Thorn across his desk, he said, "I think it's time you told me more about that fella Spotted Wolf tried to describe."

Thorn reached inside his jacket, palming the Vienna telegram as he replied, "I played a hunch but didn't tell Lute what I planned to do. Fact is, I sent a wire to Dr. Gregor Mendel in Vienna, Horst Müller's old teacher and mentor. They worked together at the university after he graduated, before coming to the States and landing here."

"And what's that you got there?" asked Win.

"The answer I received from Dr. Mendel."

Cowan took the telegram from Thorn and scanned it silently, lips moving as he read. When he was done, Win dropped the flimsy Western Union paper on his desk and said, "No love lost between them two."

"Nothing you could hang a charge on, though," Thorn said.

"Nor even get a warrant from the circuit judge, I'd bet."

"Brisbin was right in saying that professors often squabble over small things, turning friends to bitter enemies for life. The odd thing: when I mentioned Dr. Mendel to Müller, he wouldn't say a word against him, only that consulting him would be a waste of time, since Mendel only studies plants."

"What do you think this Mendel meant by 'matters shared in confidence'? It sounds to me like he thinks Müller's jumped the tracks but doesn't like to say so, if he promised not to spill it."

"I could chase that further," Thorn said, "but it means more telegrams to the Vienna university, and that means wasted time before we get an answer, if we ever do."

At that, Josiah Walker spoke for the first time since they had reached the marshal's office. "It is also possible," he said, "that Mr. Müller deviated from what Dr. Mendel sees as normal study after he departed from the school. They may have argued over methods or intentions, causing Müller to go off and work alone."

"Makes sense," said Cowan. "Come and try the New World for a change, eh? But after he got to New York City, what 'n hell would bring him all the way down here?"

"Someone should ask him that," Thorn said.

"Okay. Let's head out there right now. If he's mixed up in all this shit that we've been goin' through—"

"He'll have his guard up," Gideon cut in.

"I don't like waitin'," Cowan said. "If he's behind these killin's somehow, what's to stop him runnin' off tonight and startin' up all over, somewhere else?"

"I see it this way," Thorn replied. "He's either guilty, or he's not. If so, we still don't know exactly *what* he's guilty of."

"He told you he's been tamperin' with little ...dammit, whatever you call 'em."

"Embryos," Thorn said. "The larval stage of animals."

"All right. I never had a head for science, but we both heard Spotted Wolf talkin' about creation, yeah? He called this man of mystery—assuming that it *is* Müller—the 'father' of these goddamned things. Now, what's that mean to you?"

Thorn didn't like where this was headed, but he realized that he'd been halfway there already, in his mind, even before they talked to Spotted Wolf.

Josiah Walker picked up on it and wasn't afraid to speak his mind. "If he created the creatures we met tonight, now one of them is dead. He may fear that examination of it may lead back to him somehow, or he may simply want revenge. What would prevent him making more of them?"

"Shit fire!" Win's face was twisted, whether by outrage of fear, Thorn couldn't say. "We don't know that there's only three of 'em—or two, now that your people kilt the one." To Walker, he explained, "Our sawbones has a way of measurin' their bite marks, figurin' their size from that. Last time I talked to him, he reckoned there was three or four of them *at least*."

"And if they breed..." Josiah left the rest unsaid, for their imaginations to complete.

"I don't know nothin' about bats, except they fly around at night and eat bugs,"" Cowan said. "But if they're anything like mice and rats, they'd pop out litters like there's no tomorrow."

"We have rats out on the reservation," Walker said. "If they aren't killed first, they begin to breed at five or six weeks old. From copulation to the birth of young requires about three weeks, producing up to fourteen pups, although more commonly it's half that many."

"Christ!" Cowan was counting on his fingers, face screwed up in concentration. "Seven little monsters every three weeks—hell, say even once a month—and that'll give you...what? Like, eighty-odd a year?"

"From females, hypothetically. But if—and it's still *if,* remember—Müller found some way to make these things from scratch, he'd be the only man on Earth who really knows."

"We gotta stop him," Cowan said.

"And I'd remind you that we don't know if he's *doing* anything."

"I aim to find that out."

"But if you barge in there tonight, then what? Suppose you don't find anything. What then?"

"Well, then..."

"And if you *do* find something, what's the charge to hold him on? I stopped short of law school, but I never heard of any statute on the books against trying to breed new animals. Your cattlemen keep doing that with their imported bulls and heifers, not to mention horses, even dogs."

"Point taken, but I ain't seen any dogs, cattle, or horses that go round suckin' the blood from folks."

"Let's take another leap, since we're just speculating here," Thorn said. "Suppose Müller produced some kind of hybrid creature and it's killing people, what's the charge? What happens if a man's horse, bull, whatever, runs amok and hurts or kills someone?"

"If it's an accident, he might get sued for money," Win replied. "If it's repeated, like a wild bronco or savage dog, the animal would be destroyed."

"And then the owner moves away, if he feels like it..."

"And starts up his shit again. Okay, I get it," Cowan said. "I still come back to stoppin' him for good."

"But there's a limit to the law," said Gideon.

"I ain't so much concerned with that, right now."

"As marshal—"

"As a man who's seen one of his best friends in the world killed by these things," Cowan corrected him.

"I know the feeling," Thorn replied. "But if you take the wrong man down, regardless of your good intentions, you could wind up serving time in Yuma Prison at the very least. More likely, you'd be hanged."

"Your white man's justice is confusing," Walker said.

"You got that right, *amigo*," Cowan told him. "And we've got a gap the size of the Grand Canyon between so-called justice and the law. A fella like this Müller, livin' in a big house on a lotta land, no job except his research, as he calls it, you can bet he'd hire the best attorney in the territory, likely beat whatever charge I laid against him if it went to court."

"That would depend upon the jury," Thorn observed.

"He'd prob'ly get it moved to Phoenix, where the jurors never heard of what we're going' through, or else they think it's all a pack of lies."

"You'd have the bat, or whatever it is," Thorn said.

"Whatever's left of it by then," Cowan replied. "And who's to say for sure where it come from, or if Müller had anything to do with it?"

"We'd have to catch him at it, then," said Thorn.

"We?" Cowan echoed.

"I signed on to do a job. It's not done yet."

"Okay. So, catch him with at least one of them things, and if he's breedin' 'em, go on from there. If we could prove he sent 'em out to kill folks or their animals on purpose, he'd do time for certain. Maybe even stretch a rope."

"And your idea of how to do that is...?"

"How's this?" the marshal asked, then forged ahead. "I'm havin' that thing carted back to town tomorrow mornin'. How about we make the first stop-off at Müller's place? I'll tell him all what happened on the rez tonight, ask his opinion as to where a thing like that comes from and how it got here, when nobody in the territory's ever seen or heard of one before."

"Surprise him," Walker chimed in. "Throw him off his game."

"That's it, exactly," Cowan said.

"Of course, he'd only be surprised if no one's briefed him on what happened, yet." Thorn turned to Walker, asking, "Do you know if he has any contacts on the reservation?"

"I can say he's never been there personally," Walker said. "Some members of the nation go into Montana Camp on rare occasions, but if anyone has ever come back mentioning this Müller, I am unaware of it. Nor, would I say, is Spotted Wolf, who knows most everything that happens on the reservation."

"Right, then," Cowan said. "I'll have the carcass fetched early tomorrow and pay off the teamsters, so they aren't drawn any farther into it. We'll run it out to Müller's place before deciding what to do with it after."

"I'm trying to imagine who else needs to look at it. Lute spoke of sending off the tooth we found to Texas A.M.C., since there's no college in the territory yet."

"How 'bout a vet?" asked Cowan.

"Maybe, but we know already it's a mammal, something like a giant bat unknown to science—or, at least, it hasn't shown up in the journals yet."

"Could it be somethin' like they call...what is it? Prehistoric?" Win inquired.

That took Thorn's mind to Texas and the flying dragon he'd encountered, unearthed at another mining town, but that had been a solitary specimen sans progeny, reptilian, and it had died belatedly at his own hands.

"One giant bat, maybe," he granted, "but I can't see anybody finding three or more of them in varied sizes, which implies some older than others."

"All right. And when we spring the goddamned thing on Müller," Cowan said, "what then?"

"Depends on what he says and how he acts, I guess," Thorn answered. "If he seems amazed or just bewildered, it could mean he's innocent—"

"Or else a top-grade actor, eh?" Win finished for him.

"Yes. Or that."

"Which brings us back to how we handle it if we decide he's lyin', or whatever."

"That 'whatever' covers lots of ground," said Gideon. "If he breaks down confessing, then you've got due cause to lock him up, at least until your circuit judge decides what kind of charge will stand, if any."

"That ain't likely though, I'm thinkin'," Cowan said.

"I'd say it was a long, *long* shot," Gideon readily agreed.

"And if he says he knows nothin' about it, he can't tell us anything and sends us packin' with the carcass?"

"Without a search warrant, we'd have no option but to hit the road."

"Damned law again," Win said, shaking his head.

"The white man's burden," Walker quipped.

"Ain't that the ever-lovin' truth."

A rapping on the office door brought all three heads around, just as an adolescent runner in the garb of Western Union cracked the door and peered inside. "Marshal?" he uttered, in a voice that hadn't altogether finished changing yet. "Got you a telegram from Tucson, here."

"Come on, then," Cowan answered, brusquely.

Seeming hesitant, the boy entered, advanced, and passed the standard envelope to Cowan, waiting for a second, till the marshal said, "I'll have to tip you later."

"Yessir." Looking disappointed, the runner withdrew and shut the door.

Cowan opened the envelope, removed and read its message, lips moving again. When he was finished, he announced, "Sheriff Shibell. Says he'll be comin' down tomorrow late, or early on the eighth. Bringin' a couple of his people with him. Aims to 'sort it out,' now that he's left us hangin' all this time."

"We'll still have time to see Müller before the sheriff gets here," Thorn suggested. "Even if we don't learn anything from that, you'll have the animal to show him."

"And he won't like that, I guarantee," said Cowan. "Likely just tell me to burn or bury it and say the problem's solved."

"Surely he couldn't be that foolish," Thorn replied, regretting it almost before he spoke the words. In his experience, rural lawmen saw what they chose to see, while city cops were often on the take from criminals, or else were criminals in their own right.

"You mean because we saw two others flyin' with the one that's dead? He'll likely claim that you 'n I are both hysterical or we were drunk and seein' double."

"And the other people on the reservation?" Thorn asked.

"I predict he'll brush it off by sayin'—no offense, now, Mr. Walker—that they're 'just a bunch of Indians,' and who'd believe 'em anyhow?"

"If that's true, you should run against him in the next county election. Negligence like that, all by itself, should turn voters against him overnight."

"You'd think so, and you'd lose. He goes where money leads him, and he's friends with Johnny Behan from Yavapai County, if that tells you anything."

"Sorry," Thorn said. "I never heard of him."

"Behan was sheriff up there till about four years ago. His wife divorced him for spending his time with whores, so he resigned and got elected to the Territorial Legislature. Moved up to Phoenix with his mistress, Josephine Marcus, the actress. In his spare time, Behan likes to hang around the Cowboys—not honest cowpunchers, mind you, but a gang of rustlers, back-shooters and bandits led by Curly Bill Brocius out of El Paso and wherever else he's found to steal and raise some hell."

"I'm guessing they won't be among the men he's bringing down tomorrow or the next day."

"Keep your fingers crossed. With Sheriff Charley, you can't count on anything."

"It's always nice to know the law is on your side," said Gideon.

"Speakin' of that, I'm packin' heavy when we go out to the doctor's *hacienda* in the mornin', just in case."

"Agreed." Thorn turned to Walker, asking, "Will you stay in town tonight, to save a ride back in the dark and get an early start?"

"No place to sleep, unless it's at the livery," Walker replied.

"We can improve on that, I think. By my count, half the hotel's rooms are empty, at the very least."

Cowan chimed in, saying, "No Mexicans or redskins welcome at the Copper Queen," then nearly blushed under his tan and added for the second time that evening, "no offense intended."

"I'm accustomed to it. And no drinks at any of the three saloons."

"I can't speak for the taverns, but I likely could prevail upon the hotel's manager," Thorn said.

Josiah shook his head. "He has a boss to answer to, and someone's bound to raise a fuss."

"Disgraceful."

"Anyway, I don't mind riding back alone," Josiah said. "If I meet something in the dark, maybe we'll have another carcass for your Dr. Müller and the sheriff."

"Just don't make it yours, eh?" Win said, managing a smile that didn't suit his face.

"This way, I'll help stand watch over the animal and come back with it early in the morning, if the teamsters turn up."

"If they don't," Cowan replied, "I'll see they never haul another load out of Montana Camp."

"Until the morning, then," Josiah said, rising. "And thank you for eliminating one of the *monstruous* that have terrorized my people."

"With any luck," Thorn said, "they'll all be gone tomorrow, or the next day."

"Won't be soon enough for me," Cowan agreed.

Walker left Cowan's office, closed the door softly behind him, and faded into the night. Win studied Thorn's face and said, "Don't worry, eh? He knows this territory inside out, better 'n any white man I can think of. Hell, our cavalry hires Indians to scout for 'em, make sure they don't get lost out on patrol."

"Right now, that's not as reassuring as it should be," Thorn replied.

"Ya know, it just occurred to me we never got that supper Spotted Wolf invited us to share."

"We got a bit distracted," Thorn recalled.

"Damn right. But could you eat?"

"The truth?" Gideon said. "I'm starving."

"Good. I'll cover something for us at Delmonico's."

Thorn checked his pocket watch and asked, "This time of night?"

"They don't close up until the last dog's hung."

"Uh-huh. I'm hoping we won't find it on the menu."

"Shouldn't be, but just in case, if you pick stew, don't ask 'em where they got the meat."

Thorn forced a laugh at that, retrieved his Winchester, and followed Cowan out, after the marshal swapped his Yellow Boy for a twelve-gauge. "I loaded it with dimes this morning," he explained. "They'll cut a good-sized man in two."

"If you don't miss."

"With this, a blind man couldn't miss," Win said.

"The only other question, then, is whether it can kill a giant bat."

"I'm hopin' that we don't find out."

"Amen to that."

And as they walked down to the restaurant, between streetlamps Thorn wished had been put up at closer intervals, he found that he was hungry, after all.

But likely not for stew.

FOURTEEN

MARCH 7, 1877

Thorn had learned to sleep wherever and whenever there was time available, rarely disturbed by dreams, and wake when it was necessary, give or take a minute, without needing anyone to rouse him. On this Wednesday morning, he was up, shaved, dressed and ready well before the Mother Lode opened at six o'clock.

Before leaving his room, he eyeballed the main street and saw Win Cowan talking to a pair of teamsters with a wagon parked outside the marshal's office. They were nodding as he gave instructions, then drove off, presumably bound for the reservation, while Win ducked inside and out of sight.

Still watching, Thorn saw the first customers admitted to the Mother Lode and went downstairs, then out across the street to join them. Being early helped, as it turned out, since only the two diners who'd preceded him were there to see him enter, plus Freckles, the same waitress who had served him on his first time at the restaurant.

Was he imagining a more relaxed feeling inside the dining room, or was it just too early and too sparsely occupied to judge? Thorn wondered if the news of last night's killing on the reservation had been filtering through town, and if so, did the people of Montana Camp somehow believe their worry had been killed off with a single flying predator?

If so, he feared a disappointment was in store for them.

He ordered coffee as per usual, together with the chef's take on an "Arizona omelet" that turned out to be three eggs enfolding cheese, mushrooms, and spicy green peppers. It came with bacon, fried potatoes, and a sliced tomato on the side, all of it still hot from the grill when it arrived, except for the tomato, which was cool and fresh. It filled Thorn nicely, and a second cup of coffee black swept any small remaining cobwebs from his mind.

Before he'd finished, eight or nine more diners came into the restaurant, some of them eyeing Thorn with the suspicion he had learned to take for granted in Montana Camp—hell, anywhere he stopped for long in small towns where some local Hell on Earth had broken loose. Oddly, it came to him this time as a relief of sorts, as he'd been hoping that the gruesome cargo coming from the rez that morning wouldn't be mistaken for a cure-all to their recent troubles.

Back out on the street, he saw shops opening as usual, some merchants sweeping off their sections of the wooden sidewalks, getting ready for their day. Around the crack of dawn, he'd heard more wagons leaving town and headed up Bear Valley toward the mines, carrying workers from their humble homes to spend another day in darkness underground.

Thorn didn't ask himself if that was worth it, if forever

digging ore by lamplight constituted any kind of life at all. Each man presumably decided his own path—or if he felt forced into it somehow, it was because he lacked the gumption to break loose and seek his fortune somewhere else.

Win Cowan was emerging from his temporary office once again when Thorn approached, taking his time. A round trip to the reservation in a two-horse wagon would consume at least an hour, plus whatever time might be required for loading up the monster's carcass, covering it with a tarpaulin, and picking up Josiah Walker for the ride back to Montana Camp.

"Guess neither one of us slept in today," said Cowan, when Thorn came in range to speak without shouting. "You ready for whatever happens next?"

"As ready as I'll ever be," Thorn answered. "It could still go either way, you know."

"I'm hopin' Müller tips his hand somehow and I can bring him in. Or if he wants to play it rough, that's also fine."

"As long as we don't go in on the prod and make a mess of it."

"Don't worry. I'm on top of it, not gonna botch this, I can promise you."

"At least we ought to have a fair jump on the sheriff."

"Yep, unless his telegram was just a lie to catch me unaware. He'll want to put his own man in the job down here, soon as he can."

"Let's see how this turns out, and what your people think about it afterward."

"Phil Rutter's gonna count against me, even though I wasn't marshal when it happened. Sheriff Charley doesn't care much about details, but to hell with that. You got room for another cup of joe?"

"Guess I could manage it."

Another hour slipped away, by Cowan's wall clock, till the wagon with its grisly load returned. Josiah Walker rode his own horse, flanking the conveyance so he wouldn't have to eat its trail dust. Exiting the marshal's office, Thorn was pleased to see the carcass shrouded by a sheet of canvas, fastened to the wagon's sideboards with stout twine.

"We'd better have a look at it," Win said, walking around behind the rig.

One of the teamsters hopped down from his high seat, loosening the slipknots on one corner of the tarpaulin to peel it back, making a sour face and stepping well back from the wagon as he did so.

"Damned thing's goin' ripe," he said.

That much was indisputable. Josiah and his fellow tribesmen had prevented scavengers from feeding on its body overnight, but it was swelling from decomposition underneath the morning desert sun, and there was nothing they could do about the flies that buzzed around under the canvas, rising from beneath it when its carcass was revealed. The creature's bullet wounds, together with its eyes, lips, and the gash inflicted by a tomahawk all teemed with maggots, snacking avidly on putrefying flesh.

"Looks like a rude awakening for Dr. Müller," Win said, with a twisted smile. "Might even spoil his breakfast, if we ain't careful."

"A quick stop by the livery, and let's find out," Thorn said.

"Sooner the better, in my book." Cowan paid off the teamsters, promised to return their animals and wagon soon as he could manage it.

Thorn headed for the stable to retrieve Shadow, seeing faces behind shop windows on his way, wanting a glimpse of what lay rotting in the wagon but afraid to venture out and view it for themselves.

There was no way to ride downwind of their malodorous cargo. Marshal Cowan drove the wagon, with his Winchester and shotgun both together on the seat beside him. Thorn and Walker rode beside it, staying far enough to one side that they weren't compelled to constantly beat back a swarm of blowflies.

Moment's later, when they got to Müller's place, the wrought-iron gate was closed for once, its latch secured, but with no lock to stop Cowan from climbing down and opening it for the wagon to pass through. The house was quiet, but for pigeons strutting on the roof and cooing to each other. Thorn saw nothing of the doctor or his manservant, but smoke was curling from a brick chimney he guessed must serve the kitchen stove.

"Be ready, gentlemen," Cowan advised his two companions, as they crossed the open yard and reined in at the porch.

Thorn didn't know who readied Müller's meals, but maybe it was Pablo, or he might've had a cook on the payroll. In any case, the man himself came out to meet them moments after they pulled up, as he had done when Thorn rode out last time, alone.

This morning, Müller was attired in navy blue, same setup as before: a vest that matched his trousers, shoes that looked spit-shined, the same pince-nez, same decorative bolo tie. Thorn briefly wondered if the doctor even owned a suit coat to accompany his other dressy clothes, then scratched it off as one more thing he didn't really care about.

"*Ist* early for an unexpected visit, *ja?*" the scientist remarked, smiling with what appeared to be actual bonhomie.

"We brought something you maybe oughta see. Give us your thoughts on what it is and where it come from, if you'd be so kind," Win said.

"Something good-sized, from what I see," Müller replied. He sniffed the morning breeze, then pulled a sour face. "Good-sized and *tot,* I think."

"If that means 'dead,' you got it right," said Cowan, drawing the tarpaulin halfway down the wagon's length before he let it drop.

"*Mein Gott!* This...this...monstrosity, where did you find it, gentlemen?"

"It found us, Doctor," Win replied, still speaking for the group. "We took a ride out to the reservation yesterday, lookin' to hire the services of Mr. Walker, here, and this showed up, together with a couple of its playmates."

"There are more?"

"Two more, at least, and likely others, too. Before, I only saw the one that kilt Lute Brisbin as it flew away. I wanna say it was tad smaller than this one, but not much."

"*Mein Gott!*" the German doctor said again. "This *ist* fantastic, eh?"

"I woulda picked another word for it," said Win.

So far, Thorn couldn't tell if Müller was a fair-to-middling actor, or if he had truly never seen the beast before. Intrigued, he said, "So, Doctor, is there any chance that you can tell us what it is, or was?"

Müller stepped from the porch and closer to the wagon, seeming fascinated by the creature, breathing through his mouth to minimize the impact of its stench. Up close, he leaned in for a better look, focusing on the monster's ruined face and teeth revealed by drawn-back lips.

At last, he said, "Clearly, some sort of mammal, with a likeness to the common bats, but so much larger. As you know, my field of expertise is not paleontology, but I have read enough to say that we have nothing from the fossil record to suggest a bat species or ancestor of this size ever living on the planet."

"Still, it's here," the marshal said. "Not *living,* but it came on pretty spry last night, believe me."

"*Ja, ja.* This is quite remarkable," Müller replied. "You have a true exciting find here, gentlemen."

"Thing is, we need to track the rest of 'em and kill 'em off before they come around, drainin' the blood from any more people or their livestock."

"*Ich verstehe.* Yes, of course, I understand," Müller agreed. "Those teeth! They match the one you showed to me, eh, Mr. Thorn?"

"As close as can be," Gideon agreed.

"Clearly designed for the precision work of feeding on their chosen diet."

"If you want to call the way they kill people 'precision, Doc. I'd call it butchery."

"Of course, to layman's eyes. But from a purely scientific view—"

"I've heard about a so-called vampire bat that's fairly common south of here," Thorn said. "Much smaller, though, from what I understand."

"Oh, *ja,*" Müller replied. "*Desmodus rotundus* is the most common species. Two more are called *Diphylla ecaudata* and *Diaemus youngi*, ranging from your Mexico southward to Argentina, I believe. All three are tiny, when compared to this...this giant."

"Sounds like you know quite a bit about them," Cowan interjected, "for a guy who only studies worms and such."

"Not *only* worms, Marshal. I have a thorough grounding in zoology, as you might well expect."

"Oh, sure. So, can you tell us anything at all about this thing? I don't mind guesswork, come to that."

"Alas, beyond what I've already said—it is a mammal that resembles an enormously inflated bat—further enlightenment awaits dissection of the subject."

"Scratch that, Doc. I have to put this thing on ice if I can find enough in town, and keep it for the county sheriff when he finally comes down to look it over."

"Ah, so your superiors shall now become involved. I see."

"I don't know if I'd call our sheriff my *superior*, but he outranks me, and behind him stands the governor of Arizona Territory, though I couldn't swear he knows a thing about all this, as yet."

"Do you expect that troops shall be involved?"

Cowan half-turned to Thorn, sneaking a sly wink to him out of Müller's sight. "Well, now, I wouldn't rule it out. We kilt one of the ugly bastards, but there's three or more still waitin' somewhere in the neighborhood, for night to fall and fresh blood to be served."

Müller nodded, frowning. "I understand, of course. A primal fear evokes response from politicians who must serve the herd mentality."

"I doubt that we'll have any cattle voting in the next election, Doctor," Win responded, either playing dumb or just not getting it.

"Cattle?" Now Müller shook his head and fanned the air in front of him with one plump hand. "I'm saying that it would be most unfortunate—*nein,* tragic—if a new species unknown to man should be wiped out before we understand them, eh?"

"I understand enough to know they'll slaughter anyone they come across and leave their bodies drained like bugs that a tarantula's been suckin' on. That's all I need to know, before I start in killin' 'em."

"But you, Marshal, are not a scientist!"

"I give ya that, and probably a good thing, too. If I was more inclined to breedin' 'em, let's say, protectin' 'em, we'd soon run outa human beings in the territory."

"Predictably, that is your point of view. Perhaps if someone like myself could influence the sheriff or your governor..."

"Don't stake your hopes on Governor Safford. Sure, he's an educated man, likes buildin' schools, but he likes stayin' on the good side of his public, too. A few years back, his first wife left 'im claiming that he caught a dose of clap from some saloon girl, brung it home to her, and all. The legislature had to pass a bill allowin' his divorce. O' course, he signed it into law right smart and found himself another missus. That's out governor."

"Your sheriff, then," said Müller.

"Now, you might be onto somethin' there. Fact is, in case I didn't mention it before, he's comin' down to see us, either later on today or in the mornin'. Just to show I ain't a total philistine, I'll personally tell 'im that you wanna have a word with 'im. How'd that be, Doc?"

"You know this word? The philistine—or *Spießer*, in my native language?"

"Well, I never heard that second one, but I've been known to read the Good Book, ever' now and then."

"So, you are, in your own way then, an educated man!"

"Don't sell the country short, Doc. That'd be a bad mistake."

"*Ich verstehe,*" Müller said. "That means I understand."

"I'm learnin' all kinds of malarkey standin' here," Win said.

'What *ist* 'malarkey'?" Müller asked.

"Means good stuff," Cowan told him smiling. "Never mind. Since you can't help us with this bat-thing, I'll just haul it off before it stinks your whole place up and find someplace to hold it for the sheriff, when he gets around to us."

"I sincerely wish I could have been more helpful, Marshal."

"Sure, sure. A man knows somethin' or he don't, and no point fakin' it. If it was up to me, I'd gladly let you chop this beast up anyway you like and see what comes of it, but as I said, it ain't my call."

"Of course. Where do you plan to take it now, if I may ask."

"The only place that comes to mind," Cowan replied, "would be the icehouse west of town. It ain't too far from here, in fact, set back from the main street so people passin' through won't have to see it, but it ain't too hard to find. Might have to twist an arm or two before I get approval. The saloons won't like their ice comin' with hair and bloodstains on it, but if I start throwin' Sheriff Charley's name around, they oughta fall in line. It ain't like we'll be packin' any more monsters in there, is it?"

"I should hope not, Marshal."

"You and me both, Doc. Well, we'll get outa your hair now. Take it easy, yeah?"

Win whipped the canvas back, concealing most of the

putrescent form beneath, and scrambled back into the driver's seat beside his guns. Thorn and Walker backed their horses clear while Cowan slowly got the wagon turned around and pointed toward the gate. Nearing his destination, he called back to Müller on the porch, "Just have your man Pablo shut this behind us, would ya? Thanks again, Doc!"

Thorn waited until they were securely out of earshot before asking Cowan, "Icehouse? Are you serious?"

"As cancer," Win replied. "We stash it there until the sheriff gets to town, and in the meantime mount a close watch on the place. If our suspicion about Müller's right, he'll wanna snatch the carcass back somehow, before the territorial officials get a whiff of it. And when he comes..."

"We'll be there, waiting for him," said Josiah Walker.

"Right you are." Win smiled at both of them, asking rhetorically, "Is that a plan, or ain't it?"

"It's a plan, all right," Thorn granted.

And he was already hoping that it didn't blow up in their faces like a charge of dynamite.

FIFTEEN

MONTANA CAMP

Cowan was right. The icehouse wasn't hard to find, though Gideon had overlooked it absolutely during his five days in town. Built of bricks all painted white—to help reflect the desert heat, Win said—its walls were thickly insulated and contained a kerosene-powered refrigeration mechanism using liquefied ammonia by the smell of it, a method pioneered by England's Michael Faraday in 1820.

Standing in the blockhouse, goose flesh rising on his arms and neck, Thorn saw there would be little room in which to store their rotting monster carcass, but it should be cold enough to keep until Sheriff Shibell arrived.

Or until someone tried to steal it back.

"Suppose he doesn't come?" Josiah Walker asked, when they convened at the icehouse, an hour prior to sunset.

"Don't know if *he* will," Cowan replied. "But seein' him around, I know he's got a Mexican that does for him."

"Pablo," Thorn said.

"The very same. And there's no reason why he can't hire

others for a bit of piecework when he needs it. Patchin' up that roof of his, keeping the weeds outa his cactus garden."

"Moving dead things," Thorn concluded.

"That's my hope."

"And if nothing comes of it?" Gideon inquired.

"Like I told ya before," the marshal answered. "We give him till midnight, more or less, then sneak out there and have a quiet look around his place."

"He could leave sooner," Walker said. "Leave us behind, all sitting here."

"I reckon that he'd wanna make it late," Win said. "Fewer people to see him that way and work out which way he's gone."

"My vote would be for Mexico," said Thorn. "You can't go after him down there."

"Would you?"

"If I could prove him guilty? Probably."

Win nodded, saying, "Might go with ya. Specially if I don't have a job once Sheriff Charley gets to town."

"Let's deal with first things, first," Gideon said.

"Suits me."

Cowan had brought fried chicken from Delmonico's, cooled off from sitting in a paper bag, but edible. They washed it down with a canteen of water shared between Thorn and the lawman, while Josiah Walker balked at that and sipped his own.

Aside from food and drink, they'd all come armed with rifles—two Winchesters and Josiah's Colt—revolvers, and sharp knives that Thorn hoped would be left out of the fight. Assuming that there *was* one, and they weren't wasting their time on guard for thieves who never came.

While they were eating, conversation dropped off to occasional whispers. Thorn let his mind feel out the desert night: a hungry dog somewhere nearby, packrats scuttling around the fringes of Montana Camp—and, yes, a few small bats, likely the residents of some nearby abandoned mine, soaring aloft in search of tiny flying prey. Each animal he touched in turn acknowledged him somehow, most of them startled, pondering communication with some creature that they couldn't see or hear outside their heads. Most reticent of all, the bats—likely the small brown ones whose range spanned North America—seemed to accept his mental touch reluctantly but offer nothing in return.

From school, Thorn knew that bats comprised Earth's second largest order of mammals, about 20 percent of all the globe's known mammals. That included something like a thousand catalogued species, likely with many others yet to be discovered in the wild. They lived on every continent except frozen Antarctica, most small, but reaching wingspans of five feet or more in "flying foxes" of the tropics. Nearly all of them, except the Western Hemisphere's vampires, ate fruit, pollen, insects, or other creatures smaller than themselves.

But now there seemed to be a new and deadly breed at large, and was it thanks to Müller?

Thorn suspected it, but still refused to jump the gun and stand in judgment of a man whose oddity, his *foreignness,* made him an easy target for unhealthy prejudice.

Gideon's mind was drifting when an elbow dug him in the ribs and Cowan hissed, "Somebody's comin'." Thorn half-turned to rouse Josiah Walker, but he found the tracker already alert, holding his rifle at the ready.

Through the dark in front of them, Thorn saw a figure moving in the shadows now. The sliver of a crescent moon offered some light, but Gideon made out no details of the new arrival as he slunk between two rude frame dwellings, creeping toward the icehouse. He had only an impression of dark hair, dark skin, and black clothing, but from the figure's size surmised it could be Dr. Müller's manservant, Pablo.

"See 'im there?" Cowan whispered.

"Got him," Thorn answered back in kind.

The prowler came ahead by fits and starts, his stealth making it obvious he had no lawful business where he was. The watchers waited for him—Cowan fidgeting a little, Thorn and Walker more composed—until the man in black had reached the icehouse, looked around one final time, then opened up its insulated door to peer inside. He struck a match, confirming that the cold room held what he had come for, then shook out the light and called out softly to the darkness farther back.

"*Venga! Ser rápido!*"

Win leaned in close to Thorn, saying, "That means—"

"Got it," Thorn cut him off.

Two more figures emerged from darkness on the street's far side and joined the man who'd summoned them. *Makes one for each of us,* thought Gideon, as the sneak thieves slipped into the icehouse.

The plan was to arrest them as they left, presumably lugging the monster's carcass Win had wrapped in canvas to assuage complaints from the icehouse proprietor. It took a while, but soon enough the black-clad trio shuffled from the building, shoulders hunched under their burden, muttering what Gideon took to be Spanish curses.

"Okay, now!"

Win Cowan led the rush, raising his voice. "Stop!" he commanded. "Drop what you're carryin' and raise your hands. Make goddamn sure they're empty."

Frozen for a heartbeat, one of the burglars whispered

something to his comrades, then they all drew pistols, muzzle flashes printing bright specks on Thorn's retinas. He chose the middle target, aiming low, remembering that someone must survive to answer questions about whomever they served. If none of them was Müller's Pablo...

As a pistol slug hummed past his ear, Thorn fired and saw his target stagger, clutching at his abdomen before he turned and vanished into darkness at a lurching run. His cohorts stood their ground, still fighting back with shots wide of the mark.

Josiah Walker's Colt spoke up, a solid *crack,* his target vaulting over backward and remaining motionless after he hit the ground. Cowan squeezed off a shot that winged his man, then fired again before the gunman had a chance to flee, drilling his back.

Together, Thorn and his companions rushed their fallen adversaries, kicking pistols out of reach. It didn't matter to the man Walker had shot, already dead before he fell. The other one was wriggling, moaning, crying out in pain as Cowan rolled him over with a boot.

The lawman struck a match and held it low between the supine prowlers. Both men were Hispanic, in their late twenties or early thirties, neither of them Pablo from the Müller *hacienda*.

"Take their guns and leave 'em here," said Cowan. "They ain't goin' anywhere, and I don't wanna lose the other one."

"He's hit," Thorn said.

"You sure?" asked Cowan.

"Positive."

Without a lamp, they couldn't find a blood trail, but if Pablo or whoever held to the direction he'd been moving when last seen, the path would take him straight to Müller's gate. Pursuing him in haste, albeit with due caution, Thorn wondered if they would find that gate open tonight, or barred against them.

It was open, giving Cowan pause as they stood staring at the doctor's house, its windows dark, no lights at all visible from within. Stating the obvious, Win said, "Blacked out. They could be watching us right now."

"There's only one way to find out," Thorn answered, jogging forward, moving at an angle toward the southeast corner of Müller's abode. When no one fired at him immediately, Cowan and Walker closed in behind him, long guns at the ready.

They had nearly reached the wide veranda when a shot rang out, missing all three of them but passing close enough for Thorn to feel its breath. He ducked, then dropped behind the water trough he's noted on his prior visits.

From inside the house, a voice he didn't recognize called out in Spanish, "*Vete! No tienes nada que hacer aquí!*"

"We're goin' nowhere, Pablo," Cowan answered back. "That *is* you, ain't it? We damn sure have business with your boss."

Another shot flashed from inside, and Walker tried to peg the shooter but had no clear target in the dark, behind the stucco wall.

"*Hör auf damit!*" the master's voice called out in German, then shifted to English. "Stop! You don't know what you're doing!"

"We know plenty," Win Cowan replied. "We're takin' you in for a raft of murders. Whether that's alive or dead is up to you."

"I cannot leave my children, my creations," Müller called.

"Children, my ass!" the lawman shouted back. "They're monsters, just like you."

"*Nein!* They are tokens of the future. Can't you see it?"

Thorn began to circle, creeping, toward the south end of the doctor's home. If he could find another point of entry there, or even at the rear...

"Future, is it?" the marshal's sneer was audible. "With manmade monsters killin' people for their blood?"

"Provincial fools! While Mendel plays with beans and corn, hoping to feed the world, imagine all the benefits of animals increased in size: sheep, cattle, poultry. Think of it! A planet without hunger."

"Ya wanna tell me why ya started off with goddamn vampire bats?"

"You wouldn't understand the science, Marshal. Can you not, at least, admit that to yourself?"

"Try me."

Thorn half imagined Müller's weary sigh of resignation, like a parent dealing with a slow child, but at least he wasn't shooting now. Thorn reached the corner, slid behind it, and felt safe at last to stand. As he picked out another door, likely serving the kitchen, Müller's voice still reached him loud and clear.

"Bats were the next step after mice."

"So, you got giant mice in there with you?"

"No, Marshal. I used them to feed the bats."

"Well, sure. Makes perfect sense," Cowan replied.

"*Bow kann ich einen Idioten unterrichten?*" Something about trying to teach an idiot, Thorn understood. "Please try to grasp the basics, eh? All bats share certain units of inheritance, the building blocks of life. I owe Gregor Mendel for *that* discovery, but he lacked courage to extend his work beyond plant life. Of course, he tried to talk me out of meddling in God's domain—his foolish words. How are his various experiments with crops so different from mine?"

"One thing," Cowan replied. "I never seen an ear of corn kill anyone and suck their blood."

"There is no progress without sacrifice, Marshal."

Thorn tried the door he'd found, surprised when it opened before him, proving out his theory about access to the *hacienda*'s kitchen. Once inside the house, leaving the door open behind him, Müller's voice was clearer, amplified. Cowan's in turn, seemed smaller as he answered, "Sacrifice, is it? I get what your old friend meant about playin' God."

"Cretin! It was so *simple,* nearly child's play for a man of intellect and pure determination. I decided to experiment with bats from tropic climates, scientifically cross-breeding them: the larger species for their size and stamina, vampires for cost-efficient sustenance."

"You mean killin'," Cowan retorted.

"Do you think about where steaks and pork chops come from? Your fried chicken, maybe? Do you even care?"

"That's diff'rent."

"To the animals slaughtered on your behalf? I doubt that very much Marshal."

"Your monsters still kilt *people,* Müller."

"There is no advancement without loss.'

"I won't grieve losin' you a bit. Why blood, for Christ's sake?"

"Ah! You see? For *Christ's* sake *ja*? What is your fine religion but a cult of blood? Your preachers say it washes off your sins. Some sects pretend that when they drinking the sacramental wine, it actual turns to blood. You're all vampires, Marshal, and *cannibals* if you believe the so-called holy wafers all turn magically to flesh."

"Keep talkin', Doc. A judge is gonna love this, if you ever go to trial."

"The blood is *food*," Müller tried to explain. "Imagine how much grain would be required, sustaining herds of giant cows for meat and milk, eh? I simply devised a simpler, better way."

"Then, what?" asked Win. "People line up to eat your bats instead of pigs and cows?"

"They are more economical to raise," said Müller. "And the people of our world eat stranger things, *ja*? Snails, raw shellfish, monkeys in the tropics, eh? And living monkey *brains* in oh-so-civilized Japan. Do you enjoy a plate of so-called Rocky Mountain oysters, Marshal? What are they but testicles from bulls or rams?"

"Never tried 'em, myself."

When Thorn heard that, he had already cleared the kitchen, easing down a hallway toward the living room.

"*Mein Gott!* Why am I even wasting time on you?" asked Müller. "Where is Mr. Thorn? At least he graduated from a decent university."

"I'm right here," Gideon advised Müller.

Gasping, the German spun to face him, holding some kind of short-barreled revolver that Thorn didn't recognize.

"Ah, very clever. Or am I simply a fool?"

"That's not the question now," Thorn said.

"Oh, no? *Vas ist?*"

"Where do you keep the other bats?"

"Beneath our very feet," said Müller, smiling. "My laboratory and collection occupy a basement running full-length underneath the house. At feeding time, my children pass through double doors resembling a storm cellar's. Of course, they know their home and come back before sunrise."

"How many?" Thorn asked.

"Six to begin with, after various mistakes, but only five now, thanks to you."

"Happy to help. Have they been breeding yet?"

"Three males and two females remain. Alas, results from that phase of the project have been...disappointing."

"Something you left out of the equation, Doctor?"

"Possibly. But rest assured, I'll do it properly next time."

"You think there'll be a next time?"

"I would bet my life on it—or yours."

Before he got the final words out, Müller fired his pistol without aiming, nearly striking Gideon in spite of that. Before Thorn could return fire, Müller sprinted through a doorway to his left and disappeared.

Gideon moved to follow him, calling to Win and Walker through the front room's shattered window, "Get in here! He's running for it!"

"Comin'," Cowan answered from the yard.

Thorn turned to follow Müller, but another man lurched toward him, rising from behind a couch where he'd been huddled, out of sight. He half-gasped, "*Te mataré*," brandishing a wicked knife at Gideon

Thorn recognized Pablo, his black shirt blood-drenched from a gunshot to his side. Instead of shooting him again, Gideon lashed out with his rifle's butt, cracking Müller's servant across the jaw, knocking it out of joint. As he was falling, Thorn clubbed him again, behind one ear, putting him down and out.

Thorn ran on toward another door, standing ajar, and flung it wide, ducking in case Müller responded with a shot.

No gunfire greeted him, just stairs descending into darkness broken by a candle's fitful light.

Müller *did* fire another shot as Thorn descended, missing him by inches. Gideon fired back without aiming, and suddenly, wild screeching turned the basement to a hellish echo chamber. Ranged against one wall, iron cages stood with doors agape, the dark monstrosities inside already squeezing out toward freedom. On the far side of the basement, facing east, Müller was grappling with a heavy-looking set of double doors.

"Give up, Müller," he warned. "You're done."

"*Noch nie!*" the madman shouted back at him. "Never! You may murder me, but my creations shall survive!"

Thorn shouldered his Winchester, aiming at the enemy who still clutched a revolver, even as he shoved one of the matching doors open onto the desert night, but as Thorn's finger curled around the rifle's trigger, darkness given flesh and form erupted from one of the cages, wings unfurled.

Thorn swung in that direction, but the keening bat had launched itself at Müller, either failing to identify him or forgetting in the moment who he was. Müller spun to confront it, wide-eyed in panic, the pince-nez slipping from his nose.

"*Nein! Halt!*" he bleated. "I am your—"

The bat plowed into him, enfolded him with leather wings, it's maw fastening onto Müller's throat. His plea became a gurgling, drowning noise.

Thorn fired into the creature's back—once, twice—then turned his rifle on the others as they tumbled from their cages, chattering. Somewhere above him and behind, Win Cowan called out down the stairs, "Thorn? What 'n hell is goin' on?"

"Fetch lamps," Thorn hollered in return. "We need to torch this place."

Two of the bat-things had turned toward his voice, advancing in a kind of shuffling crawl, using their partly folded wings as arms. Thorn shot them each in turn with his Winchester, saw them slump and stagger from the head shots, then a final scream from Müller brought Thorn's eyes back to the doctor and the first bat he'd released, grappling before the open half-door to the cellar.

As Thorn watched, the monster seized ahold of Müller's neck with lips and fangs, shaking him like a terrier will shake a rat. The doctor's scream died in his ruptured throat, a gout of crimson bursting free before his head sagged over toward his right shoulder, his stout neck nearly bitten through.

"Jesus!" Win Cowan shouted from the stairs. Thorn back-pedaled to join him and Josiah Walker, just then reaching the ground floor, each with a burning lamp in one hand and a rifle in the other.

"Hurry up!" Thorn urged. "Don't let them get away."

Both men lobbed their lamps overhand, one toward the door, where Müller's bane was feasting on him now, the other toward the cages lined against the other wall. Both lamps burst on impact, spewing their fuel as it caught fire and quickly spread, flames leaping up the basement walls and fanning out across the ceiling overhead.

They fired a few more rounds into the bats still showing signs of life, then bolted up the stairs and through the house as it began filling with smoke. Cowan and Walker grabbed Pablo from where he'd fallen when Thorn bludgeoned him, one clinging to each arm, and Gideon followed the three outside into clean air.

After depositing Müller's manservant in the yard,

unconscious still, they stood and watched the *hacienda* going up in flames. Thorn couldn't tell if he heard dying bats shrieking in terror from the basement, or if it was simply wooden beams surrendering to cleansing fire. In either case, he didn't care to know.

About ten minutes later, they heard horses galloping their way and turned to find three riders pounding toward them. Farther back, townspeople were approaching in clusters, babbling among themselves while Müller's house began collapsing inward on itself.

"Here's Sheriff Charley," Cowan said, watching the foremost of the new arrivals rein his mount in to a walk.

"What's going on here?" asked Shibell.

"Solving a case," Win said. "Nice you could make it, though."

Frowning, the sheriff said, "I'm taking over now."

"You're welcome to it," Cowan said, pausing to prod unconscious Pablo with the muzzle of his Winchester. "You'll want to question this one and remember he was an accomplice to the whole damn thing."

"*What* thing?" Shibell demanded.

"Tell you all about it in the morning," Walker said. And then, to his companions, "Either of you want a drink?"

"I wouldn't mind," said Thorn.

"Saloons won't serve me," Walker said.

"Screw them. I got a bottle in my desk. If anyone don't like it, they can go to hell."

EPILOGUE

MARCH 8, 1877

Gideon Thorn was packing up his gear, preparing to depart Montana Camp, when rapping on the door of his hotel room took him by surprise. He'd said good-bye to Cowan over breakfast at the Mother Lode, Josiah Walker long gone to the reservation, and he answered now with one hand on a holstered Colt—feeling a trifle foolish as he saw the Western Union boy standing before him with an envelope in hand.

"Another wire, Sir."

"Right." Thorn handed him a dollar, took the smile the kid responded with, and locked the door behind him. Slit the envelope with his boot dagger and returned the blade to its scabbard before he opened up the telegram. It read:

> BOSTON: OBI MAGORO SENDS—HOPE ALL IS WELL. HAVE WORD FROM CHICOT COUNTY, ARKANSAS, OF DINAH PILCHER. WORKING ON A STORY THERE SAID TO BE "STRANGE," NOW MISSING. NO CONTACT WITH

COUNTY SHERIFF OR EDITOR OF "LAKE SHORE SENTINEL" NEWSPAPER SAID TO BE COLLABORATING WITH HER. LEAVING IT TO YOUR DISCRETION FOR INVESTIGATION. O. M.

"What the hell?" Thorn muttered to his silent room, no answer coming back to him.

He didn't have a clue what Dinah had been working on, or why she'd be in Arkansas of all places, but "strange" had a foreboding ring to it.

"Leaving it to your discretion for investigation," Gideon read the last line aloud.

Like he had any choice in the matter.

He might've parted company with Dinah, or else she with him, but Thorn hadn't stopped caring for her. If she was in danger, while chasing a matter like those he studied on his own, Thorn saw no choice at all.

He had to help, if that were possible. And if it wasn't...well, he'd stay until he learned the reason why.

And if someone—some *thing*—had done her any harm, there would be hell to pay.

A LOOK AT EMPTY GRAVES BY MICHAEL NEWTON

Some graves are never meant to be opened.

When Dinah Pilcher—journalist, occult investigator, and Gideon Thorn's former companion—vanishes while chasing a story in the swamps of Arkansas, Thorn sets out to find her. Her last known pursuit? A rash of grave robberies tied to whispered legends of dark rites and unnatural resurrection.

What he uncovers is far worse.

In a forgotten corner of the South, Thorn crosses paths with a brutal outlaw clan and a shadowy cult said to command the dead. Their ancient rituals promise vengeance and power—at the cost of defying the natural order itself. With every step deeper into the backwoods, Thorn draws closer to the truth... and to a horror that refuses to stay buried.

To save Dinah—or avenge her—he must face the boundary between life and death, and the monstrous ambitions of those who would cross it.

AVAILABLE MARCH 2026

THANK YOU

Thank you for taking the time to read *Night Flyers*. If you enjoyed it, please consider telling your friends or posting a short review. Word of mouth is an author's best friend and much appreciated.

Thank you.
Michael Newton

ABOUT THE AUTHOR

A California native, Michael Newton published over 215 books under his own name and various pseudonyms since 1977. He began writing professionally as a "ghost" for author Don Pendleton on the best-selling Executioner series. With 104 episodes published to date, Newton nearly tripled the number of Mack Bolan novels completed by creator Pendleton himself.

www.ingramcontent.com/pod-product-compliance
Lightning Source LLC
LaVergne TN
LVHW040220110826
845146LV00005B/1347

* 9 7 9 8 8 9 5 6 7 6 0 7 3 *